Total Eclipse of the Hex

CRESCENT MOON MYSTERY #6

TARA LUSH

COVER DESIGN BY MARIAH SINCLAIR

EDITED BY THE AUTHOR BUDDY

MAP ILLUSTRATION BY SARAH WAITES

CYPRESS GROVE
FLORIDA
Coven House
Oliver's House
Bicentennial Park
Marigold Wentworth Boardwalk Park
Police Station
POLICE
Ice Ice Baby
Haunted Hearth
HAUNTED HEARTH
Astral Attic
Astral Attic
Library
PUBLIC LIBRARY
Crescent Moon Inn
Enchanted Eternity Park

One

I had imagined this moment a hundred different ways over the past nine months, but none of those scenarios involved introducing my quirky life to my daughter while wearing a flower crown and dressed in what was essentially a muumuu.

The look on her face wasn't just skeptical. Jenny, my twenty-one-year-old pride and joy, was staring at me as if my arms had transformed into tentacles,

That expression had been stuck on her face for a couple of hours now, ever since she surprised me at the Summer Solstice festival in downtown Cypress Grove.

We were now at the Crescent Moon Inn, the bed-and-breakfast I'd inherited from my long-lost aunt. I'd imagined my daughter being delighted by the place, but instead, her eyes were filled with skepticism. She had that slight wrinkle in her nose that translated to, "*really, Mom?*"

I'd seen that look most recently when she was a senior in high school, and I'd made the grave mistake of calling her *pumpkin* in front of her friends. Tonight's faux pas was far more serious, though.

"So that was the inn's lobby. This obviously is the library, as you can see from the shelves and you know, the books, and here's the apartment where I live." I tried to remain sunny as I pulled out the mechanical hardback that opened the hidden bookcase door. "Isn't this a cool entrance? Aunt Shirley outdid herself with this. Check it out. Snazzy, right?"

She opened and closed her mouth a few times. "Uh, yeah, I guess?"

I stifled a frustrated sigh. As much as I was thrilled to have her here, this was not the way I wanted to introduce her to my new — and in my opinion, much improved — life. From the moment she walked up to me at the festival, she was in disbelief. Shock. Confusion.

Understandable, really. She had just discovered her mom was a witch. Among other things. Okay, it was also the first time she'd seen me kissing a man since I divorced her father. That had to be unsettling.

As we entered my living room, a woman's gravelly voice called out. "Amelia? Oh, Ms. Matthews? There you are! The AC in room 204 is making that rattling sound again."

I poked my head out to see one of my guests fidgeting in the doorway of the library. I smiled at her. "Oh dear. Thanks for letting me know. I'll get to it shortly."

I turned to Jenny. "Sorry, I need to handle this. It's kinda the downside to owning an inn. I'm always on call. But feel free to make yourself at home. I mean, this is your home, too. Freddie's around here somewhere, I'm sure he'll want to see you."

"Mom, I'll be fine."

We stood in the middle of my cozy living room, staring at each other awkwardly. A thick tension hung in the air, almost as heavy as my guilt. I wanted our old relationship back. One of laughter, good-natured mother-daughter banter, and pure trust.

I studied her for a beat. Jenny was like a polished version of my younger self, with her slicked-back bun and minimal makeup. Unlike her, I'd never dreamed of achieving that effortless "clean girl" aesthetic she'd clearly perfected and often talked about during our phone calls.

Her nostrils flared for a millisecond, a sure sign that she was unhappy.

Oh, dear. This was going from bad to worse. That she was even here, a month before her planned visit, was a shock. Jenny was normally a steady and even-keeled soul. She attended university in Arizona, had a part-time job at the campus bookstore, and loads of friends. Since she went away to school, I'd never once had an inkling of trouble.

She'd been scheduled to visit me next month, in late July. That's when I intended to tell her about my new powers, the coven, even about Oliver, my boyfriend. But she knew everything now, in the most abrupt manner and the worst possible way.

And yet, why had she come to Florida early? It wasn't an issue; I was thrilled to see her. My door would always be open for my daughter, no matter how old she was. Still, why hadn't she called first to give me a heads up? Nothing made sense.

My maternal instincts were on high alert. Something was definitely up.

I longed to give her another hug, but something told me to hold back. I pasted on a smile.

"Let me help the guest, then I'll put on some tea and snacks. How about that?" I tried to tamp down the feeling that I'd done a grave disservice to our relationship. I had to make it right, somehow.

"Okay," she said hesitantly, her gaze landing on a thick, leather-bound book that said the word GRIMOIRE in elaborate gold leaf script on the cover.

I hustled out before I could over-explain.

I found Mrs. Henderson from room 204 and checked the AC unit, which needed a filter change. Then the newlyweds from Wisconsin wanted recommendations for late evening cocktails (I sent them to the Grape Escape, owned by my friend Adam and his boyfriend Jason), and the Thompsons requested extra towels. My phone rang, and I answered. No, we didn't have any vacancies at all next week, and yes, the pop-up dining experience happening here tomorrow night was sold out.

Then I received a text from Oliver.

> Hey, everything okay? I feel terrible about Jenny. She looked really freaked out at the festival when she saw us together.

I quickly typed a response.

> It's definitely awkward and tense. I feel horrible about everything. Still haven't found out why she's here early. I'm trying to clear the deck of some guest issues before I have a heart to heart with her.

> Good luck. Call me if you need anything, I'll be there in minutes. Love you.

I blew out a breath. As much as I wanted Oliver at my side, I knew I needed to talk with Jenny alone. This was possibly the most serious moment in our relationship. A quick check of my smartwatch showed that thirty minutes had flown by since I left Jenny alone in my apartment. *Oh, crap.*

I practically sprinted back to her. When I opened the door, I found Jenny curled up in an oversized armchair, my cat Freddie Purrcury sprawled across her lap like a furry orange throw blanket. She was scrolling through her phone while absently scratching behind his ears, her perfectly moisturized skin glowing in the light of the antique Tiffany lamp. Looking at her in her crisp white tank top and flax-hued linen pants, I saw my own features reflected back at me, but fresher. More curated. Younger.

Sometimes it was startling to see a copy of yourself, one that was more put together than I could ever hope to be. It also made me immensely proud that she was so organized. Maybe I was once that way, too, but motherhood, marriage, and midlife had blown that façade to bits long, long ago.

"Sorry that took so long," I said, trying to sound casual despite my racing heart. "I see you found Freddie. Or rather, he found you."

Jenny looked up from her phone. "He's such a good boy. Aren't you, Fred? You're much more social than when I last saw you in California. You aren't hiding under the bed this time."

"Well, you're family. He probably remembers your scent from when I brought those boxes from home, er, California. C'mon in the kitchen."

At the word *kitchen*, Freddie jumped down to follow me, probably hoping for a second dinner. Jenny followed as well.

I started filling the electric kettle. "What kind of tea would you like? I have that vanilla chai you used to love. Do you still like that? I also have chamomile with melatonin, a special blend made by a friend with some mugwort, and—"

"Mom," Jenny said, her voice carrying that tone that told me she was about to tell me something serious. "I don't want anything with the name *wart* in it. We need to talk about what I saw at that festival. And this whole..." she gestured vaguely around the apartment, which was decorated in what I jokingly called "early hippie witch."

"This whole situation." She grimaced. "It smells like health food store in here. And not Whole Foods. The funky kind with all the bulk bins."

I took a whiff. To me, it smelled faintly of patchouli and vanilla. Maybe a hint of bread dough. Pleasant.

I set the kettle on the burner and turned to face my daughter. This was it. The conversation I'd been both dreading and hoping for. "You're right. We do need to talk. But I'd like to know something. Why are you here a month early? And how did you know to find me at the festival?"

She heaved a sigh. "I came here first and two of the guests told me you were at the park with a local witch group."

I racked my brain, trying to figure out who knew my schedule. "Which guests?"

"In their thirties, I'd guess. Tall Black guy with glasses, short white woman with a pixie cut."

"Oh, the Andersons, Marc and Sarah," I said, relieved. Since the couple had been here off and on for a couple of weeks, they'd become practically like family. I had mentioned the festival to them. "They recently got married and are on their honeymoon."

"Yeah, well, I figured you'd be selling cookies or something, but there you were... *dancing*."

She shook her head, as if to erase an awful memory. Still, one mystery answered.

Now to get my other question resolved. "And why are *you* here—"

Jenny cut me off with a shake of her head. "It's a long story and I'd rather talk about *you* first."

I opened the fridge and focused on the contents, wondering how I should react. I was the parent here, not her. And yet, I knew that seeing one's (divorced) mother kissing a random man and swaying and chanting in a public park during a summer solstice festival was a lot to take in. So I let her words slide and pulled out a bowl of unbaked cookie dough.

"You always have the cookies ready," Jenny observed, only now there was a faint smile on her face. "What kind are they?"

"Basic chocolate chip, but I've added a lavender sugar twist," I said.

"Mmmm. That sounds good. At least your baking skills haven't changed."

The familiarity of this moment hit me hard, and my eyes threatened to fill with tears. How many times had I baked cookies with Jenny over the years? From the time she could reach the counter while standing on a step stool, she'd been at my side. I remembered her at five, her little fingers covered in dough as she tried to shape cookies into hearts "for extra love," she'd say.

She'd always dunk them in milk, waiting a beat too long until the cookie threatened to break apart. I stifled a wistful sigh.

At least this was a starting point for our conversation. No one could focus on an empty stomach, and the sugar would help us power through. I took out a baking sheet and parchment paper, and began scooping the dough into small mounds.

The recipe was a local one, from Dorothy Thompson's gravestone in the Enchanted Eternity cemetery, which was known for the recipes carved into the headstones. Although, I wasn't about to tell Jenny that detail. My daughter was barely handling the solstice festival.

Learning that my latest cookie recipes came from grave recipes would have to wait a day or two.

I sprinkled a pinch of lavender-infused sugar atop each cookie. "I'm sure you remember how my Aunt Shirley, your great aunt, died and left me this inn?"

"Of course, and that she left Uncle Mike the condo in North Carolina."

"South Carolina."

"Same thing."

My daughter was such a West Coast girl. We'd have to work on her southeastern U.S. geography.

"Okay, honey, this is going to sound a little weird, but hear me out. Shirley had abilities."

She screwed up her face. "Like...?"

"Extranormal abilities."

Jenny threw up her hands. "What do you mean by that? She read tarot cards? Looked into crystal balls?"

"Shirley was a witch. She was part of a coven. She could talk to spirits, too."

Jenny took a moment to rub the back of her neck. "Uh-huh. Sure. Go on."

"When I arrived and found out these details, I was super skeptical, exactly like you are right now. Trust me. Shirley left me instructions, though."

"Like, how to run the inn?"

"Yes, that, and how I needed to deal with a certain situation here in order to make the inn profitable."

Her eyebrows shot up. "Yeah, okay..."

"There was a ghost here in the inn, and he was causing trouble, and I was the one who needed to help him." I tried to say this casually, as if I'd hired a plumber to fix a problematic water heater. I continued for a few minutes, telling her about Billy the ghost, how he'd turn off the air conditioner in the middle of the Florida summer, and explained the use of my newfound psychometry to solve his cold case murder. I became more animated as I talked.

"And then we held a séance and he was able to cross over to the other side without any issues." The corners of my mouth turned up at the memory. It had been the first time I'd had an inkling of what my true powers entailed.

Jenny stared at me, horrified, while I slid the cookie sheet into the oven. "A ghost. Really? And psych...psychometry. What is that even? Mom. Maybe we need to get you in to see a professional. I find all of this extremely jacked up."

"I know it sounds crazy," I said, setting the timer. "But it's real. I can touch things and often glean details, visions of events, even emotions. Remember how I used to get attached to things, like my wooden spoons, and how they preferred to be in a special container? I almost anthropomorphized the silly things. Or when you were a kid, and I'd make up stories about your stuffed animals, how they had past lives? I've been thinking about those times, and I believe that was a precursor to my current powers. But I never listened to my intuition."

Because I was too busy being a wife and mother, I wanted to add.

"Mom, that was you being charming." She folded her arms across her chest. "And organized."

I leaned against the counter. "No, sweetheart. I mean, yes, I suppose I can be charming. And mostly organized. At least I used to be. But I've always had this ability. Moving here made it stronger. Like it was awakened at midlife. That's what the witches here have taught me."

Her eyebrows shot up. "The witches?"

"Cypress Grove is different. Special. It's the Psychic Capital of the World."

Jenny snorted. "That's a marketing slogan. To draw tourists here."

I took a deep breath. "Which brings me to what you saw at the festival. Those women? They're my coven."

She rolled her eyes. "Oh God. No."

"The Sisters of Hecate. We're a coven for Generation X women. We do spells, help the community, study magic. And sometimes…" I hesitated, then decided to go all in. "Sometimes we solve murders. Well, I do. And a few of my coven friends. Others in the group have different skills, or stick to, say, bake sales or plant seedling swaps."

I had to admit that I sounded a little unhinged, and licked my lips. Suddenly, I felt a tad feverish. Maybe I should hold off on telling her about the murder I'd recently solved, of a man who dropped dead while we were playing on the coven's pickleball team.

"Murders?" Her voice cracked. "Mom, are you hearing yourself? This sounds certifiable. Like, completely bananas. Now I'm super worried. I think you've lost it. Did you join a cult? Is that what this is? Because I saw a Netflix series about women who move to small towns and get sucked into weird—"

"It's not a cult," I interrupted firmly. "It's a supportive community of women who practice real magic. Remember the woman with the red hair? The one next to me at the festival? She can cast protection spells. And Amy, she can walk through walls using shadow magic. And Renee—"

"Stop." Jenny raised her hand. "Just… stop. This is too much. Way too weird. I'm tired and jet lagged and I can't believe this is even happening."

There was an awkward pause. Finally, she broke the silence. "Does Gramma know about this?"

I rubbed my lips together. My mother was well aware of my new life. She'd visited a few months back and not only had met

Oliver, but had tagged along on a coven mission to take down a rogue witch. I should probably save that story for later.

"She does," I said after a pause.

"Unreal," my daughter cried, slapping her hand on the table, the sound sending Freddie galloping out of the kitchen. "So two people in my family kept this from me. Or you've both gone mad. What about Uncle Mike?"

"No. I haven't told him yet." My brother probably would have little trouble believing I'd joined a coven. In fact, I was certain he'd find it hilarious and even fitting. "I was waiting to talk to him in person. Like I was with you."

The timer dinged and I pulled out the perfectly golden cookies. The scent of vanilla and melted chocolate filled the kitchen, and I slid one onto a plate and set it in front of Jenny. "Here we go. Nice and warm, exactly as you love them."

She focused on the cookies for a long moment, then glanced up at me, her expression wary. "Are they magic cookies? Do they have cannabis in them?"

I pressed a hand to my chest. "Weed? Of course not. No, they're regular cookies. Though Jimbo, he works here at the inn, says they have plant energy because I use specially sourced Madagascar vanilla."

"I thought Jimbo was the front desk guy-slash-handyman? Isn't that what you told me on the phone?"

"He's that. And a plant shaman, too."

Jenny dropped her head into her hands and groaned. "And who was the dude you were kissing? Wait. Don't tell me. Some kind of warlock? Or a wizard? A Dungeons and Dragons master? Or is he a random guy who watches Lord of the Rings marathons on weekends?"

"The *dude* is named Oliver Everhart. He's a tenured professor at a local university," I said, pausing. Probably it was best not to tell her that he was a world-renowned professor of paranormal history in Florida. "Also an author. He has no psychic abilities, and he's a wonderful, brilliant man. We are, um, hanging out. Hooking up. Hanging out and hooking up all over the place."

Jenny's eyes popped out. "You're hooking up? You're not exclusive? What do you mean? How many other—"

"No, no, no." I waved my hands. "We're exclusive. We're dating. Like old people. Sorry. Terrible phrasing. My bad."

I set more cookies on the plate between us and poured the tea. Jenny dunked a cookie into her tea and took a bite. Her eyes closed briefly in appreciation.

"These are exactly how I remember them, but the lavender sugar is a nice addition," she said, then fixed me with a look while dunking her cookie again. "So. Oliver. How long has that been going on?"

I got the distinct impression this was a safe topic.

I busied myself with stirring honey into my tea. "Well, we met the first week I arrived. We were friends for a while. So about seven months, I'd say."

"Seven months?" Her cookie broke off into the tea and she let out a small grunt of exasperation. Her eyes flashed at me. "And you didn't think to mention your relationship during any of our calls?"

"I told you I had friends," I said, wincing at how inadequate that sounded. "But it never seemed like the right time on the phone. It was far too serious for a call. Plus, you were dealing with finals and then that whole drama with changing dorm rooms."

"Mom." Jenny set down her cookie with deliberate care. "You found time to tell me about Freddie's new cat tower. And your neighbor's granddaughter's viral video on YouTube. And that time a guest clogged the toilet three times in one night." She ticked each item off on her fingers. "But somehow you couldn't squeeze in, 'Oh, by the way, I'm dating someone'?"

"When you put it that way..."

"And I had to find out by seeing you two *making out* at some..." she waved her hand dismissively, "witch festival? Mom, what is going on with you? First you move to this weird small town in Florida. Florida! You've never even expressed interest in this place! I thought you hated humidity and frizzy hair."

My hand drifted up to my reddish locks that had lightened in the Florida sun. Yep. It was frizzy.

"Then you start talking about ghosts and psychic powers, and now you're dancing around in flower crowns with a bunch of middle-aged women calling themselves witches?"

I felt my defenses rise. "The Sisters of Hecate are a respected—"

"Please, no." Jenny pressed her fingers to her temples. "I'm trying really hard to understand this, but you have to hear how out of pocket it sounds. Psychometry? Really? What's next? Are you going to tell me Freddie's actually a familiar?"

I glanced at the orange cat, who, at that moment, was licking himself in a particularly undignified position. He glanced up and met my gaze, as if to say, *this is all on you, sister.*

I thought back to the time that he and I communicated with an elderly ghost baker and her ghost cat, then cleared my throat. "Well, actually—"

Jenny gestured wildly, her gold hoop earrings catching the light. "Listen to yourself! This isn't you. You're practical and organized and... normal." Her glossy lips pressed into a thin line of disapproval. "You're a mom."

"Moms contain multitudes. Being practical and having psychic abilities aren't mutually exclusive," I said, trying to keep my voice calm. "And I didn't solve those murders with magic alone. I used detective work too. And Oliver helped—"

"Oh right, Oliver." Her tone shifted from worried to exasperated. "The boyfriend you never mentioned. Does he know about your extracurricular supernatural activities? Or does he play amateur sleuth with you like some middle-aged version of Charmed?"

I leaned against the counter, suddenly aware of the contrast between us — my comfortable middle-aged body in its flowing clothes and practical sandals, versus her youth and polish. But I stood straighter, remembering what my friend Liz always said about owning our power at any age.

"He teaches at a university in Orlando and does research on Florida history and folklore. He's more academic about it, but he's very supportive of—"

"Great." Jenny grabbed another cookie, but this time she merely held it, staring at it like it might contain answers. "So not only did you not tell me about him, but he's encouraging whatever this is. Sounds like the perfect guy."

She scowled at the herbs hanging from my kitchen ceiling and the crystal grid on the windowsill. There was a sigil that Oliver's sister, Sage, had carved for me out of some local tree, nearby.

"Honey," I reached for her hand, but she pulled back. "I know this is a lot to take in. But all of this — the inn, the coven, my abilities, Oliver — it's part of who I am now. I'm still your mother. I'm still me. I've merely found a new part of myself."

"A part that communes with spirits and casts spells?" She let out an exaggerated sigh. "Mom, I don't know about this. Maybe this place is having some kind of effect on you. Maybe you should talk to a therapist. Does Dad know? Have you told him?"

I snorted. My ex was the last person I'd ever call to talk about, well, anything. "I don't discuss my personal life with your father."

"So he's unaware of everything?" She let out a bitter laugh. "Geez, Mom. He probably thinks you're running some quaint little B&B by the beach."

"I don't care what he thinks. It's none of his business," I said, my tone more defensive than I'd intended. "We've been divorced for years. I don't need his approval for how I live my life. I'm not having a breakdown. Everything I've told you is real. I know it's hard to believe, but—"

"You know what? I'm tired from traveling. The flight was awful." Jenny stood while placing the uneaten second cookie on a napkin. It wasn't like her to eat only one cookie. "I think I need to lie down for a while. Process... whatever this is."

She paused. "And Mom? Next time you want to keep a secret

from me? Maybe don't. You could've at least told me about the boyfriend first, not the whole 'I see dead people' thing."

"I'm sorry. Truly. I didn't think this was a conversation to have in a text, or on the phone. I was going to tell you when you came next month. But here you are. And I'm so happy you're here." I allowed a small smile to form.

Jenny sighed, her shoulders slumping. "Um, where am I going to sleep? Didn't you say you cleared out a downstairs guest room for me?"

Oh, no. My heart sank. The guest room downstairs wasn't ready, wouldn't be ready for another month, when Jenny was actually supposed to arrive. I'd been using it as a makeshift storage space for inn supplies and some of the coven's seasonal decorations that I'd borrowed for solstice.

"Well, yes, technically," I said, hoping it wasn't as bad as I remembered, since I hadn't had time to even go into the room in a week. Or two.

"Let me see it," she demanded. Sometimes my daughter could be bossy when she was tired, and usually I didn't indulge that behavior. But I was also exhausted and frazzled and too tired to bicker, so I gave in.

We trooped out of my apartment with Freddie at our heels. Jenny winced as we made our way through the gothic-décor of the dining room to a hallway. I unlocked the door to Room 101.

Jenny peered into the room. Boxes of paper products for the inn competed for space with bundles of dried herbs and a stack of meditation cushions for guests. Three different seasonal wreaths leaned against one wall, and a few overflowing boxes of Yule decorations occupied every inch of the queen sized bed.

"Is that a cauldron?" Jenny pointed to a large black pot barely visible behind a mountain of folded sheets.

"A friend asked me to store it until — never mind." I shut the door quickly. "You can take my room. I'll sleep on the sofa. Tomorrow I'll rearrange things in here."

My mind spun, wondering if I should rent a storage unit for

all the junk. That would be easiest. Unfortunately, Jimbo, my one employee, was on vacation this week. Maybe I'd be sleeping on the sofa for more than one night.

"Mom, no—"

"I insist." I rubbed her mid-back as we walked back toward the apartment. "I changed my sheets earlier today, and there's plenty of closet space."

Jenny hesitated, then nodded, gathering her bags from where she'd dropped them in my living room. She disappeared into my bedroom without another word, closing the door with a soft click that somehow felt more final than a slam.

I sank onto the sofa, and Freddie immediately jumped up beside me. As I pulled the throw blanket over my legs, he settled into his usual spot against my hip, purring softly.

"I really messed this up, didn't I?" I whispered to him while stroking his broad back.

His only response was to purr louder and knead the blanket.

In the dark, I stared up at the ceiling, wondering how my carefully planned mother-daughter summer visit had gone so spectacularly wrong before it had even properly begun. The festival, Oliver, the coven, my powers. I'd meant to ease Jenny into all of it gradually. Instead, she'd gotten the equivalent of magical cold water straight to the face.

Freddie stretched, his paw batting at something that had fallen between the sofa cushions. I reached down and pulled out one of my crystals — a piece of clear quartz I'd been meaning to cleanse. As I held it, no psychic impressions came through. Apparently even my powers knew when to take a break. I put it on the coffee table, next to my phone.

The sounds of Jenny moving around in my room eventually faded into silence. An earlier thought hit me like a punch to the gut: I still didn't know why she was here four weeks early. Something must have happened. The urge to knock on my bedroom door was almost overpowering, but I forced myself to stay put.

Whatever it was, it could wait until tomorrow, when we were both rested.

Tomorrow, when I also had to deal with that pop-up dinner sponsored by the local Chamber of Commerce.

I pulled the blanket up to my chin and tried to quiet my racing thoughts. One crisis at a time, I told myself. The sounds of Jenny's soft snoring drifted into the room, reminding me of when she was little and would crawl into my bed after a nightmare. Except this time, I was the nightmare she was hiding from.

"Some homecoming," I whispered to Freddie. He was sleeping yet purring, completely unperturbed by the family crisis that was unfolding around him. Maybe he had the right idea.

Sleep now, and deal with everything else in the morning.

I woke at five in the morning with a crick in my neck and the kind of full-body stiffness that made me wonder if I'd aged a decade overnight.

The sofa, while perfect for an afternoon of reading with Freddie or snuggling with Oliver while watching a movie, wasn't designed for a middle-aged woman and an eighteen-pound cat to sleep on. Every joint creaked as I sat up, and my lower back made its presence known with a sharp twinge.

"Ughhh," I groaned softly.

But the physical discomfort was nothing compared to the hollow feeling in my chest. Every time I thought about Jenny's expression when I'd told her about the coven, or the hurt in her voice when she'd realized I'd kept Oliver a secret for months, I felt like the worst mother in history. What kind of mom hid major life changes from her only child?

Amelia Matthews, that's who.

Freddie chirped a greeting and stretched, completely unconcerned with my maternal crisis. At least someone had slept well.

"Come on," I whispered to him. "We've got breakfast to make."

My guests deserved their usual morning spread, regardless of my personal drama. The Crescent Moon Inn's reputation for breakfast was part of what kept us booked solid, and I wasn't about to let my emotional turmoil get in the way of perfect scones.

I crept into the kitchen, careful not to wake Jenny in the bedroom. The pre-dawn quiet of the room wrapped around me like a familiar blanket. Everything looked different in the blue-grey light peeking through the windows. It was softer, more magical. Or maybe that was my overtired brain trying to find the bright side.

First, the coffee. While it brewed, I fed Freddie before he could meow his head off, then pulled out butter to soften and preheated the ovens. The routine was soothing: measure, mix, create. Lemon-blueberry scones were first. The dough came together under my hands like little clouds. While they baked, I started on the quiche, one with spinach and goat cheese, another with mushrooms and herbs from my garden. The kitchen filled with the best scent in the world: home cooked food.

Next came the fruit salad, jewel-bright berries and perfectly ripe peach slices tossed with a few squirts of honey and fresh mint sprigs. I arranged strips of thick-cut bacon on baking sheets, and sprinkled them with black pepper and a touch of brown sugar.

By six-thirty, both the kitchen and I were toasty warm, and the dining room table was set with the inn's collection of mismatched vintage china. Crystal sugar bowls caught the early morning light, and little silver cream pitchers waited to be filled. I'd pulled the last batch of scones from the oven when I heard movement in the other room.

Jenny was awake. My stomach did a nervous flip, but I pushed the feeling aside and focused on arranging the pastries on their tiered stands. Meanwhile, the inn's ever-present to-do list crawled through my brain like the news headlines on a cable channel.

The inn was nearly full, but later this morning would be briefly quiet. Most of my guests were checking out by eleven, heading home after the Midsummer Festival. Mrs. Henderson would return to her grandchildren in Tampa. The Thompsons were driving back to Atlanta. The retired couple from Maine who'd spent the week antiquing and taking classes on astral projection would catch their afternoon flight.

Only the newlyweds from Wisconsin, the Andersons, were staying on. They'd been here off and on for a couple of weeks while traveling around Florida. This was their last stretch before going home, and were excited to be around for tonight's dinner.

The chef doing the pop-up event was scheduled to arrive with his entourage later today. I wasn't sure if he was bringing one or two people. Hopefully not more.

Normally Jimbo, my one employee, handled the bookings and would help with a dinner like this. But he was on a weeklong vacation, taking his girlfriend Sage — Oliver's sister — to a dude ranch out west to celebrate her new job and her birthday.

I heard distant footsteps on the stairs. Probably Mrs. Henderson, who had been first to breakfast for the past few days. She claimed it was because she was still on her grandkids' schedule, but I suspected she didn't want to miss out on the thick slab bacon while it was warm.

When I was in the dining room setting the breakfast table, Mrs. Henderson appeared in the doorway in a mustard-colored tie-dye dress.

"Good morning, Amelia. Something smells wonderful."

I smiled. Her genteel southern accent was so musical. "Morning! Hope you slept well. Coffee's ready on the buffet," I told her. "Breakfast will be out soon if you want to get comfy here in the dining room."

More footsteps followed as the rest of my guests came downstairs. In my inn, everyone ate at one long table. I felt it encouraged conversation and even friendship. Nothing thrilled me more than when I read online reviews of my inn, and guests wrote that they'd stayed in touch with others they'd met over breakfast.

The Thompsons chose their usual seats by the window. The couple from Maine, whose names I could never quite remember despite a week of breakfasts, settled onto the opposite end. Marc Anderson, the newlywed from Wisconsin, guided his bride to a seat, his hand resting protectively on the small of her back.

I moved between the kitchen and dining room, pouring coffee, answering questions about checkout times, and offering driving directions. The rhythm of service helped keep my mind off Jenny, at least until a young, familiar voice hit my ears.

"Morning, Mom. Do you need help?"

I turned to find my daughter standing in the doorway, dressed in yoga pants and an oversized Chico State t-shirt. I recognized it as one she'd stolen from me years ago when we lived in California. Her hair was pulled back in a messy bun — so different from yesterday's sleek style — and she wasn't wearing any makeup. She looked young. Vulnerable.

"Good morning. No, honey, you should sit down and eat," I said, trying to keep my voice steady and warm. "There's plenty of everything."

"Mom." She gave me a look I knew well, the one that said she wasn't going to back down. "You taught me to always help out. Remember the Christmas party at the Richardsons'?"

A lump formed in my throat. That Christmas had been right after the divorce, right before I'd adopted Freddie into my life. We'd been invited to a dinner party at her best friend's house, and Jenny had insisted on helping in the kitchen because "that's what Matthews women do."

"No, no, but if you really want to do something, there's a full carafe of orange juice there on the counter. You can bring that out with you and have a seat," I managed.

Jenny nodded and headed for the kitchen. I watched her go, guilt washing over me fresh and raw. Here she was, still trying to be a good daughter despite everything I'd dumped on her yesterday. Still living by the values I'd taught her about helping, even though I'd kept so many secrets.

I'd really messed this up.

"Amelia dear?" Mrs. Henderson's voice pulled me back to the present. "Could I trouble you for more of that delicious bacon?"

Right. Guests first. Mother-daughter crisis later.

Jenny moved through the kitchen with the same efficiency she'd inherited from me, refilling coffee cups and bringing out fresh fruit without being asked. When she passed behind Mrs. Henderson with the bacon platter, the older woman twisted and beamed at her.

"You must be Amelia's daughter," she said. "You look exactly like her."

"Her only daughter," Jenny replied with a smile, though I noticed the slight tension in her shoulders at the comparison.

Once everyone was served, I touched Jenny's arm. "Sit down and eat something. You must be starving."

She hesitated, then slid into an empty chair. I finally recalled the Maine couple's names and did quick introductions around the table, ending with the Andersons. "And this is Sarah and Marc, who are honeymooning with us."

"How wonderful to meet you," Mrs. Henderson said to Jenny, reaching for another slice of bacon. "We've heard so much about you. Your mother is so proud. She told us all about you making the Dean's List last semester." She leaned forward conspiratorially. "Tell me, dear, do you have the gift too? The whole town's been talking about how your mother helped solve that dreadful business with the pickleball murder recently. Such a remarkable talent, her psychometry. Everyone in town knows about it."

I nearly dropped a basket of toast. Jenny's smile went rigid, but she managed to maintain it as she shoved an enormous bite of quiche into her mouth. She chewed with deliberate slowness, then reached for her glass of juice, clearly buying time.

I jumped in. "Jenny arrived yesterday and is a bit jet lagged. She'll be staying with us for, ah, the rest of the summer." Would she? At this point, I had no idea if she'd be here two days or two months, and I feared I'd have less time with her than I wanted. "More coffee, Mrs. Henderson?"

Jenny shot me a grateful look and proceeded to demolish her breakfast with unusual speed. I kept the coffee flowing and the conversation moving, steering clear of any topics involving psychic abilities, witches, covens, or anything extranormal.

That wasn't easy, since it was the town's bread and butter, or the tarot and talisman, if you will. The extranormal was the sole reason why many, if not all, of my guests were in town (along with my breakfast, I liked to believe).

"Going to be a hot one today," I said to the room. "Make sure you all wear your sunscreen."

While my guests chatted and ate, I kept moving, refilling mugs and clearing empty plates. My stomach growled quietly, but my short time as an innkeeper had taught me to ignore hunger until the work was done (or sneak a slice of bacon here and there).

Meanwhile, the morning light hit my collection of mismatched china in a picture-perfect way, making the gold rims gleam and the rose patterns seem to dance. Why couldn't life be as simple, and as beautiful as setting a mismatched table?

Mrs. Henderson devoured the thick-cut bacon. The Thompsons always reached for seconds of my scones, and the couple from Maine had already declared my quiche "absolutely magical," though they didn't know how close to the truth that was.

Nine months of serving breakfast had taught me to pay attention to these little details about my guests, the way their faces lit up at the first sip of coffee, how conversations bloomed over a hearty meal.

Jenny caught my eye a few times, but I couldn't read her expression.

The crowd thinned gradually. Mrs. Henderson hugged me goodbye, whispering that she'd leave a five-star review and would be back for Samhain. After getting directions, the Thompsons headed out to beat the theme park traffic. The couple from Maine thanked me profusely for "the most magical week of their lives," though I wasn't sure if they meant the inn's ambiance or their astral projection classes.

Soon it was only Jenny and me in the quiet dining room. Freddie had emerged from wherever he'd been napping and was doing his usual post-breakfast inspection of dropped crumbs. He licked the floor and I gently nudged him with my toe.

"I usually start cleaning the rooms around now," I said. "You don't need to help. I know you probably want to catch up on your sleep. Oh, and I think we'll keep you in my room again tonight. Is it comfortable?"

I was dying to ask her why she was here early, but something — a mother's intuition, most likely — told me that she'd bring it up in her own time. Especially after my own communication breakdown with her, I didn't want to nag her for an explanation. She was an adult, after all.

Still, I was worried. Jenny wasn't the impulsive type.

She nodded, pulling out her phone. "Yeah, it's fine."

"If you want some fresh air, the back porch and garden is nice in the morning. The crepe myrtles are blooming, and there's a good Wi-Fi signal." I hesitated. "The coven helped plant the herb garden, but, um, it's still a regular garden, except for the sage crop, which has some special healing properties."

"Mom." Jenny's voice carried a warning tone.

"Right, sorry. I'll be upstairs if you need me."

As I headed up with my cleaning supplies, I glanced back to see Freddie following Jenny toward the porch. He seemed in great spirits, trotting after my daughter like an orange shadow, his tail held high.

The sight of the two of them together made my heart swell.

Three

By the time I finished turning over the last room, my back was aching and my shirt clung to my skin despite the air conditioning. Cleaning rooms was quite the workout, as it turned out. I'd found the usual collection of items left behind; a phone charger, two paperback paranormal romances, and a single sock decorated with cartoon ghosts. I deposited them all into the hotel's lost and found box.

At least the Maine couple's attempt at astral projection hadn't left any ethereal residue. That had happened once before, and smudging an entire guest room was not my idea of a fun morning (I'd had an assist from my dear friend Liz Lopez, who owned The Astral Attic, a witchy supply store downtown).

I found Jenny on the back porch, sprawled in one of the white Adirondack chairs with her feet propped on the railing. She'd changed into shorts and a T-shirt, and had her hair piled high on her head. A glass of ice water sat sweating on the little table near her chair, and Freddie was curled next to her, purring loud enough that I could hear him from several feet away.

The morning's relative lack of humidity was a gift, and for late June in Florida, it was downright pleasant. A breeze stirred the crepe myrtle blossoms, sending pale pink petals drifting onto the lawn.

"Hey there. Mind if I join you?" I asked.

Jenny glanced up from her phone and shrugged, which I took as permission. I sank into the chair across from her.

I took a deep breath. "About yesterday. And really, about everything. I owe you an explanation. And a huge apology. A better one than what I gave you last night."

Freddie opened one eye to look at me, then went back to sleep. Jenny's gaze flicked to me, then back at her phone.

"I need to tell you something," I began, then stopped. Started again. "When I came here—" Another pause. Freddie's purring filled the silence. How could I explain everything so she'd understand?

Jenny flipped her phone over and stared at me. At least I had her attention now. I steeled myself and tried again. "Living in Cypress Grove, it's the first time in, well, in decades, maybe my entire life that I've been living only for me. Not as someone's daughter, or mom, or wife. Just Amelia." The words tumbled out in a rush. "And I know that sounds selfish—"

"Hmm." Jenny's tone was unreadable as she stared at her phone, probably wanting to look at it but knowing I'd reprimand her. I wanted to shout, to tell her that this was crucial information. But I also knew that her phone was like a security blanket. It helped her process my words, and more importantly, her feelings. It wasn't how I handled things, but that didn't matter at the moment. And chiding her about phone use right now didn't seem like the best use of our time together. So I soldiered on.

"I felt like this place was, I don't know, my destiny. Like it was essential. Like I could finally breathe and be myself. Especially after what I went through with the divorce." I watched a crepe myrtle petal land on Freddie's orange fur. He didn't stir.

Jenny gnawed on her bottom lip. Her gaze went to the trees, then the sky over my shoulder, then at me. "You couldn't have told me this at Thanksgiving? When we had our last holiday in our California house?"

"At that point, I'd only been here a couple months," I said, remembering that awkward dinner where I'd gotten the entire meal pre-made from Safeway and tried to act like nothing had changed. "And I wasn't certain of anything. Wasn't sure what I was seeing and experiencing here was normal. I mean, it's not exactly normal, but it's become my new normal."

"Still. You could have mentioned something. Anything. I should've known something was off when you didn't make your own pie." She scowled. "Sheesh."

I shifted in my chair, chastised. Those were the early days in Cypress Grove, when I had one foot here and one in California, the period when I sold my home in Sonoma and ended that chapter of my life.

"I know. I considered it. Telling you, I mean. Not the pie. I still think Safeway makes a great pumpkin pie, you know."

She snorted a laugh.

"I wanted to explain everything on that trip. But I also wasn't sure any of this was real, so I didn't want to worry you." I was aware of her skeptical look but hurried on. "I mean, I knew it was real, but I wasn't entirely sure what to think about it all myself. How do you explain to your incredibly practical and smart daughter that you're suddenly seeing visions and joining a coven?"

"Mom." Jenny set her phone down, and I recognized that particular stillness she got when steeling herself for confrontation. It was the same way she'd looked before telling me she was quitting soccer in eighth grade. "You do realize how this sounds, right? Like, if I told you I'd joined a... I don't know, a unicorn-riding club in Sacramento, wouldn't you be concerned?"

That familiar knot formed at the base of my throat, the one that appeared whenever my daughter and I stood on opposite sides of an issue. "Unicorns aren't real," I said automatically, then winced as Jenny's shoulders drew up tight.

"But ghosts are?" She arched an eyebrow at me in a way that

was painfully familiar. It was my own skeptical look, perfected and turned back on me. Suddenly I had an inkling of how my own mother felt sometimes. *Drat.*

"And magic? Is that real?" Jenny continued. "And whatever else you've gotten mixed up in?"

Freddie chose that moment to wake up, stretch, and hop into my lap. As he settled in, I could have sworn he gave Jenny a reproachful look. His presence was comforting.

Jenny was quiet for a moment, her fingers absently tracing patterns on her pale pink phone case. "You know," she said finally, "I took this feminist literature class last semester. We read Virginia Woolf."

"A Room of One's Own?" I asked, surprised by this turn in the conversation.

"Yeah." She sat up straighter, tucking her legs under her. "We talked about how women need their own space to create, to become who they really are. Not only physical space, but mental space too." Her eyes swept over the garden, taking in the herbs I'd planted, the wind chimes Jimbo and Sage had hung up, the crystal grids catching morning light in the window. "I guess... I guess this is your room. Your space."

The lump in my throat made it hard to speak. "It is."

"And the whole witch thing, the psychic abilities. Maybe it's a metaphor. Or it's part of discovering who you are without," she gestured vaguely, "without all the roles you've had to play. That's how I'm going to think of it. Easier that way, I guess. Maybe it's a midlife thing and I won't get it until I turn forty-five."

"Maybe it is something like that," I murmured, daring to hope she was starting to understand.

"Of course some moms have an affair with the pool boy when they have a midlife crisis. Or they get really into yoga."

"A pool boy isn't exactly my style," I said dryly.

The corners of her mouth quirked up. That felt like victory.

"I still think it's weird," she said quickly, but there was less edge to her voice now. "And I'm not totally convinced about the ghost stuff. But." She took a deep, shuddering inhale. "But I get why you needed this. Why you needed to figure it out for yourself first. I think. It'll take some getting used to."

"Of course, honey. Take all the time you need."

Freddie's purring grew louder, as if adding his approval.

"Though you could have told me about Oliver," she added, a hint of her earlier irritation returning. "Having a boyfriend isn't exactly supernatural."

I laughed softly, relief making me feel lighter than I had since yesterday. "You're right. I should have told you about him. I just, I wanted to keep him in my Cypress Grove bubble for a while. Like a secret garden."

"Mom, you're getting poetic. No metaphors about your garden, okay? I remember you making that kind of metaphor when you bought me that Our Bodies, Ourselves book when I was taking sex ed." She shuddered.

I bit back a grin. "Okay."

"I actually am glad you are dating. I was worried about you after you and Dad divorced. You seemed hella lonely."

I nodded. We sat in silence for a few beats.

I shifted in my chair, causing Freddie to readjust his position with an annoyed *brrrap*. "So," I said, trying to sound casual, "are you going to tell me why you're here early?"

Jenny's shoulders tensed, and her phone came back up like a shield.

I watched her face, seeing the stubborn set of her jaw. It was another trait she'd inherited from me, one I'd gotten from my mother. I had a vague memory of being pregnant with Jenny and my mother laughing, saying something about karma.

"Not that I mind," I added quickly. "I love having you here for as long as you want."

A dozen scenarios rushed through my mind, each worse than the last. My protective instincts screamed at me to demand answers, to fix whatever was wrong.

But then I really looked at her. At the confident young

woman who'd navigated her way across the country on her own, who'd handled college with a grace I never had at her age. Who'd shown more maturity about her parents' divorce and my life changes than I'd probably deserved. She wasn't my little girl anymore, needing me to solve all her problems.

Still, I was her mother.

"Are you failing a class?" I asked softly. "Or do you need money?"

She shook her head twice while heaving a sigh, still staring at her phone.

"Did you take drugs? I mean, something harder than smoking pot?"

She grunted. "No. And nobody smokes anymore. They take edibles. It's legal in Arizona, you know."

"Good to know." I paused, then a horrific thought hit me. "Have you been arrested?"

That got her attention. She glared at me. "No, Mom. Geez."

I lowered my voice to barely above a whisper. "Are you... pregnant? Because if you are, we can work it out together—"

"Oh my word, Mom, *no*." Jenny rolled her eyes so hard I worried they might stick that way. "There's no possible way I am with child. I'm not pregnant, I haven't been arrested, and I'm not in trouble or a drug addict. Can we maybe... not? At least, not right now? I'll talk about it when I'm ready. Everything is pretty okay, okay?"

I stifled a sigh and instead forced a smile. I noticed the time on her phone screen. I had four hours until the chef and his entourage arrived, and I still wanted to show Jenny around town.

Pretty okay would have to do for now.

Now it was time to check my phone, since a notification had popped up. "Speaking of things I need to handle today, I should tell you about tonight's event. If I could cancel, I would, but unfortunately this is a big deal locally."

"The pop-up thing you mentioned?"

"Yes. The Chamber of Commerce has this new initiative to

put Cypress Grove on the culinary map. They're pairing social media chefs with local venues for these fancy prix fixe dinners." My mind spun with everything needed for tonight, when all I wanted was to spend time with my daughter. "The Crescent Moon Inn got picked for the first one."

Jenny sat up straighter. "So that's why those boxes in the lobby have 'Special Event' written on them?"

Ugh, I needed to move those before tonight. "Partially. Though some of those were left over from the coven's..." I caught her expression and knew I had to move on. "Anyway, we're hosting a small group of people tonight. The Andersons — the honeymoon couple — bought tickets, plus some local folks. I'm putting up the chef and his assistants for free, letting them use the kitchen, and I have to decorate the dining room. The Chamber said it will be an intimate dinner, kind of a trial run, so they can iron out the kinks and learn how to promote it well next year."

I tapped my fingers against my chin. "There's also supposed to be someone filming it all. Maybe a whole crew? I don't know. The email wasn't clear on that part." Or perhaps I'd merely forgotten, given that I'd solved a murder a not that long ago. Suddenly I felt extremely unprepared for it all. I pinched the bridge of my nose.

"Sounds fancy."

"It is. The Chamber wants to showcase that Cypress Grove isn't only about..." I waved my hand in the air.

"Ghost hunting and tarot cards?"

I pointed at her. "Exactly. Though I wouldn't be surprised if this chef works some kind of magical element into the meal."

Jenny gave a dramatic head toss, but there was a hint of amusement in her eyes. "Instead of farm-to-table, crystal-to-table. I'm not sure if I buy it entirely. But if I know you, the desserts will be good."

After our talk in the garden, I decided to give Jenny the tour she should have gotten yesterday, after the festival chaos. That evening's guests weren't expected for several more hours, according to their emails, so this was a good time to introduce Jenny to both the inn and the small town of Cypress Grove.

We also needed to swing by a local business that rented table linens, place settings, and other decorations for events. I'd chosen a pretty, lavender-hued summer theme, and knew it would look gorgeous in the formal dining room. They'd donated the stuff for the pop-up in exchange for me telling the guests about the service.

As we walked through my Queen Anne Victorian B&B, I explained to Jenny that the inn was almost exactly as Aunt Shirley had left it: sprawling and a bit worn around the edges, with an eclectic mix of antiques and vintage finds she'd collected over decades. Some of the wallpaper was starting to peel in places, and a few of the original hardwood floors creaked under our feet, but that was part of its charm.

"I'm planning some renovations," I said as we climbed the main staircase, running my hand along the mahogany banister that desperately needed refinishing. "Updates to the bathrooms, fresh paint, that sort of thing."

Jenny trailed her fingers along a faded damask wallpaper. "It does have character. It's super-duper aesthetic. People would kill to film this for TikTok."

We worked our way through the inn's eight guest rooms, each with its own quirky personality thanks to Aunt Shirley's decorating style. There were four-poster beds draped with vintage quilts, Victorian fainting couches, and enough doilies to supply a small army of grandmothers. There were also more witchy touches, too, like the stuffed raven on a bookshelf in room 205, or the painting of a small Victorian-era child in an elaborate dress, holding a crystal ball, in room 300.

"The best part," I said, leading her back downstairs, "is that I'm planning to expand the apartment. Work should be able to start in a month. Jimbo has friends in construction."

We passed through the library with its hidden door and into my apartment. "I have plans to add another, larger, room to this. I wanted you to have your own space when you visit, and use it also as an office."

Something flickered across Jenny's face. It was an expression I couldn't entirely read. She looked around the apartment, lingering on the herb bundles hanging from the fireplace mantel.

"A whole bedroom just for visits?" she asked, her voice carefully neutral.

"Well, yes. I mean, I know you'll be at school or working most of the time, but still." I ceased talking when she became very interested in examining Freddie's cat tower.

We then headed out to explore the town, because I wanted to treat her to my favorite iced coffee at Ice Ice Baby, my preferred java joint.

The morning's dry air had given way to typical Florida humidity, but some fluffy clouds kept it bearable. Downtown Cypress Grove was at its most charming, with its buildings painted in tropical colors and window boxes overflowing with exotic flowers.

Jenny's eyes lit up as we drove through downtown. We parked near the police station — I didn't tell her that I'd had more contact with local cops in nine months than I had in my entire adult life — and walked down Main Street.

"This is all super cute," she said, stopping to look around.

"I knew you'd love it. That's Donut Witch," I said, pointing to a pale blue storefront. "The best donuts in town, plus they do tarot readings at your table."

"Of course they do," she murmured. But instead of making a beeline for the clothing boutique like I thought she would, she focused on the clouds on the horizon for a few long seconds..

"Oh, and that's Mrs. Peabody's Pet Psychic Services," I said, pulling on her arm and gesturing to a tiny pink cottage. "She's actually wonderful, according to my friends, though Freddie refuses to see her. Says she's too chatty."

Jenny turned her attention from the sky. "Says? As in, Freddie told you this?"

I probably should have eased into this part. "No, she told me Freddie said that. He doesn't talk, of course. It's more like impressions. Though that one time with the ghost cat—"

"Nope," Jenny held up her hand. "Not ready for ghost cats." But she was fighting back a smile as we continued down the sidewalk.

I considered taking her to The Astral Attic, the New Age supply shop owned by my friend Liz. I knew she wasn't working today, or for the next ten days; she and her boyfriend, police chief Christopher Wolf, were on an Alaskan cruise.

A group of tourists passed us, all wearing matching purple t-shirts that read "CYPRESS GROVE: WHERE EVERY DAY IS SUPER...NATURAL!" One woman was clutching a large anthracite crystal.

"The tourist season is year round here," I explained.

Her eyes flitted to an event poster in the window of a local insurance business. YOGA FOR WITCHES, it said.

"Witches." She shook her head.

"And mediums, psychics, the occasional werewolf." I noticed her skeptical expression and quickly added, "That was a joke. Mostly."

We reached the town square, where people were setting up booths for one of the many summer street markets.

"I'm not sure what's going on today. I can't keep track of all the festivals and summer markets," I said.

The massive oak trees were draped with crystals that threw rainbow patterns across the grass. A man in flowing robes was doing tai chi by the fountain, and several squirrels watched him from the trees.

Jenny took it all in, her expression somewhere between bewilderment and reluctant fascination. "It's like Stars Hollow had a baby with Salem, Massachusetts, and then that baby moved to Florida and got really into crystals. And everyone wore flip-flops."

I laughed. "That's actually pretty accurate."

"And you really love it here? All of this?" She gestured at a shop window displaying ritual brooms and something called "Mercury Retrograde Emergency Kits."

"I do," I said softly. "It's home."

Jenny was quiet for a moment, watching a woman in full pirate garb walk past with a parrot on her shoulder.

"Well," she said finally, while glancing up at the sky, "I guess it's not boring."

$$\mathcal{F}our$$

By the time Jenny and I were done with downtown, the afternoon steamy heat had settled over Cypress Grove like a blanket that had spent hours in a sauna. My cotton dress was plastered to my skin, and Jenny's ponytail had developed a wicked frizz that she kept patting at absently. Even the iced lavender honey lattes we'd picked up at Ice Ice Baby hadn't been enough to completely ward off the Florida weather.

As we walked down Main Street toward the car, I noticed Jenny checking her phone, then at the clouds again.

"What's the weather app saying?" I asked, knowing her familiar quirk from when she was in high school. She'd been obsessed with checking the forecast before soccer practice. Even as a toddler, she adored watching The Weather Channel. I used to joke that after learning the words "Mom," and "Dada," her next words were "Jim Cantore."

Frankly, I was surprised that she hadn't majored in mete-orology.

"There's some kind of alert." She stared at the screen. "Severe thunderstorm warning? In the middle of the afternoon? In this heat? Wow. But those clouds look scary."

I glanced west, where dark clouds were stacking up like angry bruises. "Welcome to Central Florida in summer. The storms here aren't like anything you've seen in Arizona or California."

"Yeah, we get, like, dust storms and extreme heat warnings." She took a slurp of her iced latte. "How bad do they get here?"

A distant rumble of thunder punctuated my answer. "Bad enough that the locals know to prepare when they see clouds like that. The streets here can flood pretty quickly, especially in this downtown area. The drainage system wasn't exactly engineered for modern storms, and all the development on the edge of town has also caused some problems."

I gestured toward the antique store's doorway, where the owner was already setting out sandbags. "Everyone here has a routine and takes the storms in stride."

Jenny's eyes widened. "Seriously?"

"Mm-hmm. Usually the storms blow over quickly and the water never really reaches the businesses. It drains into the sandy soil, but sometimes the streets get snarled and you can't get anywhere for a while. I've learned to hunker down at home." I shrugged. "The inn's on high ground, thankfully. I was told by folks around town that Aunt Shirley was very particular about that when she bought it."

"Because of flooding?'

I smiled. "She told my friend Liz it was because spirits prefer elevation. I'm not sure if that's true, though."

"I believe people here would think that." Jenny snorted. "Like the linen place. The rental company really claimed their linens were cursed." Jenny asked. "Like, actually cursed. Unreal."

We were now at my car, and climbed in. We chatted for a bit about the linen company on the short drive to the Crescent Moon. My order wasn't ready, and wouldn't be. It was a slight annoyance, but in my previous life as the owner of a cookie delivery company in California, and now as an inn owner, I was prepared for anything and everything to go wrong at the last moment.

Hospitality was all about pivoting when needed.

"Apparently there was a mix-up with some ceremonial table-cloths from a lunar event." I sighed, turning into the inn's parking lot. "The woman said something about negative energy and mercury being in retrograde. Bottom line is, I have to figure out how to set the table for tonight's dinner using what I have on hand. We'll throw something together, I guess."

"Really? Mom, I can do this!" Jenny's whole face lit up. It was the most animated I'd seen her since she arrived. "I've been watching all these tablescaping videos on TikTok. We could do a whole vintage-meets-modern vibe. Mix your mismatched china with some simple greenery. Maybe add some of those crystals you have everywhere..." She stopped herself. "I mean, if that's okay? If they're not serving some other purpose."

"You want to help?" I tried not to sound too surprised. Never had Jenny showed interest in interior design. She was majoring in education, and had a goal of being a math teacher.

"Are you kidding? This is totally my thing. We could use some of those brass candlesticks I saw in the library, and—" She broke off mid-sentence, squinting through the windshield at two figures on the wraparound porch of the Crescent Moon Inn. One was pacing back and forth while the other stood perfectly still, holding what appeared to be a tablet.

"Oh, crud," I muttered, checking the time on the dashboard. "I'll bet that's the chef. He said he'd be here at four, though, and it's only three."

Jenny let out a small gasp. "Wait a second." She grabbed my arm. "Mom, that's Nico Romano."

"Who?"

"He's huge on TikTok. He does these cooking videos and..." She grimaced slightly. "He's kind of a thirst trap chef."

"A what now?"

But before Jenny could explain, the chef had spotted us and was striding down the steps, the other man trailing behind him like a shadow. Even from here, I could see the displeased expression on the man's chiseled face. Uh-oh. I'd met enough culinary professionals to know that chefs tended to have volatile personalities. This one looked like a doozy, and I hoped I was wrong.

I climbed out of the car with a big smile. "Hello there!"

"Amelia Matthews, I assume," he called out, his voice smooth as velvet. "I am *so* sorry. We arrived much earlier than I thought. I hope it's not an issue or a problem."

"Not at all. It's great to meet you." I held out my hand but he swooped in and kissed me, European-style, on both cheeks. He smelled like a powerful cologne, with notes of musk, amber, and plastic. Like something that a teenage boy would wear, not a man in his thirties (although I was a terrible judge of age as I got older). The guy could be twenty-two, or forty-five, given the rise of Botox and facial fillers.

"Plans change. You know how it is." He ran a hand through his perfectly styled dark hair. The motion caused his fitted T-shirt to pull across impressively muscled shoulders, the kind you get from hauling restaurant equipment and, I suspected, many hours at the gym. And possibly steroid supplements. "Oh. This is my assistant. Ben."

The slim young man with wire-rimmed glasses and an anxious expression cleared his throat. "Nice to meet you, Ms. Matthews. Chef, how much do you want me to bring inside?"

Nico shot him a look that could have curdled cream. "Everything, Ben." He turned back to me and his entire face softened. "Can you please show me to your kitchen right away? I need to start prep immediately. This is a carefully orchestrated seven-course experience, not some backyard barbecue. I want to do this historic inn justice tonight."

He laughed heartily, as if he'd made the best joke on Comedy Central.

My grin had turned to a tight smile. "Of course. But first, why don't you let me show you to your rooms so you can at least drop off your bags and get settled?"

"We'll do that later," Nico said with a dismissive wave of his hand. "The kitchen first. Ben can deal with the luggage."

I exchanged another glance with Jenny. I'd prepared rooms 204 and 205 for them — the nicest ones available after the honeymoon suite, where the Andersons were — but apparently Chef Romano had other priorities. I'd even set out a gift basket in each room, filled with Cypress Grove goodies, such as handmade chocolates, bags of coffee, and Crescent Moon Inn-branded mugs.

"At least let me give you the keys," I said, digging in my bag. I handed them to Ben, who accepted them with a grateful nod. "Second floor, end of the hall. 204 is yours, Chef, and 205 is for Ben."

As the assistant scurried to their vehicle, Nico took a call and turned his back to us. Well, then.

Ben loaded up a large wagon, the kind used by pro photographers and people who were serious about beach necessities. It had canvas sides and fat, grippy wheels. Jenny and I walked over and asked if he needed help.

He shook his head. "I'll be inside in a few, I have to check with Chef on a few things. Thanks, though, that's really kind of you."

I explained how to get to my apartment, and Jenny and I walked to the front door. She leaned close and whispered, "Nico's way crankier than in his videos where he spanks bread dough."

I refrained from chortling. Spanking bread dough? On the internet? Suddenly I felt a million years old and sighed. Why would someone spank dough? I was beginning to rethink this entire pop-up event. It was way too late to cancel, though, and the Chamber of Commerce had been so helpful and welcoming when I'd inherited the inn. I'd immediately said yes when they offered me the first spot of the "Dine Around Cypress Grove" event.

Like many other things in life — divorce, colonoscopies, attempting to sync my phone with my car's Bluetooth — I had to power through until the bitter end.

At least I had my daughter with me.

I unlocked the front door and, like I always did, I paused at the computer to check the voicemail. Shirley had left behind an old-fashioned machine that was probably from the late 80s, and I didn't have the heart to get rid of it. Frankly, I wasn't even sure how it was plugged in or where it connected to, since I never used a landline, and all calls went to my cell. Like many things in the inn, it was a mystery.

"Mom, what's that?" Jenny peered at me as I pressed the "play" button.

"One New Message," the robotic voice called out, followed by a long, wheezy *beeeeeep*.

"This? It's an answering machine."

She looked at it in horror. I looked at her similarly, realizing my twenty-one-year-old daughter had probably never seen one before.

"So this is the inn." Nico interrupted us and I quickly pressed the STOP button on the machine.

"Yes, this is the Crescent Moon. Come, I'll show you the kitchen."

"This is." he paused, nostrils flaring slightly. Then he sniffed. "Unexpected."

"This inn was my aunt's. I inherited it about nine months ago." I gave him a quick rundown of the inn's history, watching him take in the gothic wallpaper and my small-yet-growing collection of antiquarian spell books.

Ben trailed behind us, backpacks on his front and back, while pulling the wagon. He nearly dropped the handle when he spotted Georgina, my four-foot-high taxidermied alligator that stood on its hind legs.

"Oh, gosh. I thought that was real." Ben pressed his hand into his forehead then laughed. Jenny also giggled. They exchanged mock worried glances and laughed some more.

"Ben," Nico purred. "An alligator doesn't walk on two legs."

"That's Georgina. Isn't she fun?" I patted the creature's snout.

"Where did you find—" Ben had no sooner begun to utter his sentence when Nico gave an impatient grunt.

"I'm running late and need to begin filming. Where is the kitchen, Amelia darling?"

Jenny and I exchanged glances. "It's through here," I said, leading everyone toward my apartment. I knew something was up when neither Nico nor Ben commented on the hidden bookcase door that led to my living quarters. Usually people went wild over that decorative touch (which was also thanks to Aunt Shirley).

Once we were inside, Freddie took one look at our visitors and sprinted into my bedroom, a flash of orange fur disappearing around the corner.

I led everyone into my apartment kitchen. While it was normally the perfect size for me to prep breakfast for my guests, it now felt impossibly cramped with four adults. The inn had a second, larger kitchen, but I hadn't ever used it, and was considering renovating it into a different, all-purpose area for guests. I wasn't even sure the oven worked in there.

"Well, here it is." I waved my hand in the air. "Please let me know what you need. The Chamber of Commerce came to look and they said I had everything you'd ne—"

"Wait," Nico interrupted, looking around. His gaze landed on the stove. It was a fairly expensive model, gas range, with a grill. I adored the thing, mostly because it hit the perfect temperature for my cookies (something I suspected was a hint of magic, thanks to Aunt Shirley).

"This isn't the kitchen we're using, is it? Is there another?" He visibly shuddered.

"This is the only kitchen."

"This cannot be happening." Nico massaged the middle of his forehead with his index and middle finger. "Ben! Get me Kristan from the Chamber on the phone. Now!"

While Ben fumbled with his phone, Nico paced the small space, muttering under his breath. His expensive sneakers squeaked against my freshly mopped floor. "A home kitchen? For a seven-course tasting menu? With wine pairings?" He yanked open my cabinets, barely missing the dried lavender bundles hanging from the ceiling. "And what is all this?"

"Those are herbs," I said. "Fresh ones, actually. My employee grows them himself. He's a plant shaman, if you'd like to—"

"No." He slammed the cabinet shut. "Ben! Where is Kristan?"

"Her voicemail, Chef." Ben's voice quavered. "I've left three messages already."

"Useless!" Nico spun around, causing Ben to stumble backward into my crystal grid on the windowsill. Several stones clattered to the floor.

"I'm so sorry!" Ben dropped to his knees, scrambling to collect the fallen crystals.

"Leave them," Nico snapped. "We need to get the rest of the stuff from the car. Maybe we can salvage this disaster." He stormed out, leaving Ben still kneeling on my kitchen floor.

Jenny moved to help him. "Here, let me—"

"No, no, I've got it." Ben's hands shook as he carefully replaced each crystal. "They're in a specific order, right? For energy flow or something?"

I noticed how Ben's eyes kept drifting to Jenny as she helped pick up the fallen crystals. When she smiled at him in thanks, he ducked his head and blushed. There was something endearing about his shyness, especially compared to Nico's aggressive vibe.

"Actually, yes, they are for energy flow," I said, hoping to diffuse the tension between Ben and his boss. "Are you interested in—"

"BEN!" Nico's bellow from the doorway made us all jump. "THE EQUIPMENT WON'T UNLOAD ITSELF!"

Ben scrambled to his feet, nearly knocking over my jar of organic bay leaves. A flush came over his tanned face. "Coming, Chef!" He paused at the door and glanced at me. "I really am sorry about the crystals."

After he rushed out, Jenny turned to me. "Well, Ben seems sweet at least."

"Unlike his boss." I straightened the crystal grid, noting that Ben had actually placed them back correctly.

We heard the sound of the front door opening, followed by more yelling.

"YOU CALL THAT CAREFUL HANDLING? THAT'S A THOUSAND-DOLLAR COPPER PAN!"

"Maybe we should focus on the dining room," I suggested. "And you can tell me all about this Chef Nico and his TikTok thirsty trap."

Jenny burst out laughing. "Mom, it's thirst trap. Not thirsty trap."

I snickered. "I like my version better." I paused. "Uh, hang on, let me make sure Freddie's okay. I don't want him escaping outside with all this commotion."

I slipped into my bedroom, shut the door, and froze. In less than twenty-four hours, my normally tidy space had transformed into what looked like a college dorm room. The sheer volume of stuff was staggering. Not only clothes and toiletries for a summer visit, but what appeared to be everything she owned. I shook my head. I remember being young and not knowing how to pack for a quick trip.

Her expensive skin care products had completely taken over my antique dresser, arranged in meticulous order (morning routine on the left, evening on the right). There were dog-eared novels and an old high school yearbook from her school in California. My bulletin board was off its easel in the corner and leaned against one wall, already decorated with photos. When had she done all this?

I peered closer. Most were of people her age, but a few were of Jenny and me, and her dad. When she was younger. When we were a family.

The bed was perfectly made — some habits I'd instilled had clearly stuck — but clothes occupied every other surface. Designer jeans draped my reading chair, athletic wear spilled from my antique armoire, and formal dresses still in their garment bags hung from my shower rod that was visible through the en-suite bathroom door. A ring light stood in the corner, along with two massive suitcases.

And there, in the middle of this carefully curated chaos, was Freddie. He'd made himself at home in an open suitcase that still contained several sweaters.

Sweaters? In the summer? In Florida? Really, kid?

Meanwhile, Freddie looked pleased with his new nest. His orange fur contrasted beautifully with the pink Barbie sweatshirt that I'd sent Jenny for Christmas. He opened one eye as I entered, shot me a look that clearly said, "Don't you dare move me," then went right back to the land of nod.

"Freddie, you little meatloaf," I chided fondly, but something nagged at me as I paused to survey the room again. A flash of maternal worry shot through me, but before I could process it, another crash and bout of shouting from the kitchen reminded me of our more immediate problems.

Five

I closed the bedroom door quietly, leaving Freddie to his designer nest. Jenny waited in the hallway with her hands stuffed into her shorts pocket.

"You ready?" I asked her. She nodded and followed me out of the apartment.

The dining room was one of my favorite places in the inn. Usually, late afternoon sun streamed through the stained glass windows, casting jewel-toned patterns across the dark wood wainscoting. Today, however, there was a slightly darker light, probably because of the storms looming on the horizon. Hopefully they wouldn't be too bad, and streets wouldn't flood.

I flipped on the light, illuminating a vintage chandelier that hung from an elaborate medallion on the ceiling. The effect was both elegant and slightly eccentric, much like the inn itself.

I opened a sideboard drawer and took out a pack of organic wood wipes.

"So," I said, struggling to extract a wipe, "tell me about our chef. You seem to know a lot about him. And feel free to go through the cabinet here. It's where I keep all the linens and stuff. Shirley left so much behind that I don't even fully know what's all here. I keep to a shabby chic look for breakfasts."

Jenny opened a drawer, took out an autumn-themed table runner, and inspected it. Her movements were precise. She'd always had an eye for detail. "He got famous on TikTok during the pandemic, doing these um, somewhat suggestive cooking videos. And he also posts about his workouts. All this biohacking stuff, like drinking raw eggs with turmeric and doing ice baths. He's trying to live to be a hundred fifty."

"Biohacking?" I wrinkled my nose. "What happened to enjoying food and living life? Do people really want cooking advice from someone who drinks raw eggs?"

"His followers do. He's got millions of them."

I shook my head, feeling several steps behind today's pop culture trends. I once knew them all, back in the late 80s and early-to-mid 90s.

Jenny rifled through the drawer and found a runner that was a warm, summery green. "This is pretty."

"It is. And there are a lot of matching napkins."

"Hmm." She rifled through the drawer. "Anyway, Nico. Just, you know, tight shirts and lots of close-ups of him kneading dough. His catchphrase is 'Let's get cooking, beautiful people.'" She imitated a deep, exaggerated voice that made me snort-laugh.

She laughed too, a sound that was pure happiness to my ears.

I moved to the sideboard, surveying my mismatched china. "What do you think—the green and white Wedgwood with the rose-pattern Royal Albert?"

"Actually..." Jenny bit her lip. "What about mixing the gold-rimmed ones with those pink depression glass plates? Kind of a Lilly Pulitzer-meets-Bridgerton vibe? We could alternate them."

I paused, studying the combination. "You know what? That's perfect. The pink will pick up the sunset through the windows." I started setting them aside, while inspecting everything for chips. "So what else about Nico?"

"He's got like, millions of followers. Started with a food truck in Miami, then got super popular online." She shook out a place-mat. "But lately there's been drama. Some other chefs accused him of stealing recipes. And there was this whole thing with his last restaurant partner..."

"Drama? Do tell." I moved to my collection of candlesticks. No two were alike, all with their own histories. Some had come with the inn, a couple others I'd found at estate sales. As I picked up one, warmth shot through my fingers and suddenly I was seeing my Aunt Shirley, decades younger, using this very candlestick to chase a raccoon out of the kitchen while wearing a flower-print nightgown and fuzzy bunny slippers.

This happened often with my psychometry. I'd experience visions of my aunt's life, or other scenes from the past. Usually they were mundane, but on occasion, I'd see more disturbing things.

I must have swayed slightly, because Jenny paused in her napkin folding. "Mom? You okay?"

I set down the candlestick carefully, swallowing a laugh at the image of Aunt Shirley brandishing it like a sword. "I'm fine, honey. Just a hot flash. Perimenopause is such fun." I fanned myself with my hand, avoiding her stare. We were having such a nice moment, working together like this. No need to bring up my psychometric visions right when she was starting to relax around me.

"So anyway," I said quickly, "you were telling me about the restaurant drama?"

Jenny gave me one more concerned look before continuing. "Right. Well, apparently, the partner claimed Nico was impossible to work with."

I raised an eyebrow. "That's a shock, from what I've seen today."

"The guy claimed Nico was using the restaurant's money to fund his social media career." Jenny folded another napkin with precise movements. "Nico said the partner was jealous of his success and trying to sabotage him. It got really messy online and they trended on the For You Page. The comments were off the chain, with everyone taking sides and making duets about it. His stans went crazy in the quote posts."

I blinked at her. "I understood maybe half of those words. For You Page?"

"It's a TikTok thing, Mom. Like, what the algorithm thinks you want to see, and—" She saw my expression and laughed. "Never mind. Just think of it as internet drama. Lots of people filming reaction videos in their cars about it."

"People film themselves reacting in their cars? Why can't they go indoors?"

"Oh my God, Mom, you're so chronically offline." She grinned. "That's a compliment, by the way. Though I bet the inn would do amazing on BookTok. All these vibes. It's like a paranormal romance come to life."

Thank the stars that my generation didn't have social media when I was Jenny's age. I shook my head, arranging another place setting. "You know what? I'm going to focus on making sure we have enough wine glasses for everyone."

"Sure, Mom. Get on with your Gen X self." She patted my arm with exaggerated sympathy, but her smile was affectionate. We both snickered, but another crash from the kitchen made us wince.

"Yikes," I whispered. Hopefully Nico wasn't being too nasty to poor Ben.

We worked together in silence for several minutes. I polished the silverware with a cloth, then

stood back and watched Jenny arrange the place settings. She'd taken the forest green linen napkins and folded them into elegant fan shapes, securing each with antique silver rings. The crisp green against my white lace-edged charger plates created a fresh, summery feel.

A cream damask tablecloth was the base, then palm-green placemats arranged with mathematical precision. My aunt's silver gleamed against the verdant backdrop, while the collection of cut crystal goblets caught the afternoon sun. In the center sat a whimsical ceramic pineapple in sunny yellow and Kelly green glazing.

"It's giving coastal grandmother meets The Crown," Jenny declared, adjusting a fork that was already perfectly aligned. "Very old money aesthetic, but make it Florida."

I wasn't entirely sure what that meant, but I nodded my approval. "Beautiful," I said softly. "It looks like something from a magazine."

Jenny beamed. "The pineapple is the perfect centerpiece. It's fun but still elegant. Though Nico will probably hate it. He's more minimalist, but I think this makes more sense for, like, a summer dinner party. If you want, we could grab some foliage from outside — I saw those gorgeous pink flowers out back."

"Well, I adore it, and yeah, maybe some flowers would be a good idea." I pressed my hands into my hips. The whole table managed to be both formal and welcoming, exactly what I always aimed for at the inn. "You've made something really special here."

She continued tweaking the settings.

"Seriously, Jen, you're really good at this. The whole, what did you call it? Tablescaping?"

She ducked her head, but her pleased smile was obvious. "Thanks. I watch a lot of design videos. It's kind of become my obsession lately. Remember when I worked at that catering company last summer? I learned about setting a formal table then, and really enjoyed it a lot." Something in her voice made me look up, but she was very focused on folding and fanning a napkin.

I was about to ask her how her new job at the on-campus bookstore was going, but the sound of Nico's voice rose again from the kitchen. He yelled something about inadequate ventilation and the impossibility of achieving the proper sear on scallops. Jenny and I shared a grimace.

"Well," I said, "at least the table will be gorgeous, even if our chef has a meltdown."

"Mom?" Jenny held up two different vintage salt shakers, one silver, the other white porcelain. "Which one?"

"Your choice, honey. I trust your judgment."
Her smile lit up the room brighter than any chandelier.

Six

The sound of raised voices drew me back to the kitchen before I could stop myself. Jenny followed close behind, her flip flops making soft thwacks against the hardwood floor.

"...most expensive ingredients I've ever worked with," Nico was saying as we entered. He stood at my butcher block island, carefully unpacking what looked like a small cooler made of stainless steel. He flashed a coy smile in my direction. "Hello, ladies. This is a certified fugu master's kit. Cost more than your car, probably."

I drove a ten-year-old Toyota Corolla and also owned a beat-up white van that had been Shirley's, one that looked like a serial killer had owned it in 1983. "Most things cost more than my car," I deadpanned.

Ben hovered nearby, his tablet clutched to his chest like a shield. "But Chef, I thought we were doing regular puffer fish? The non-toxic farm-raised—"

"Don't be ridiculous." Nico's tone dripped with contempt as he lifted out a sleek case containing various knives. "You think I'd serve that tourist garbage? This is wild-caught. My contact in Miami imports it from a trusted source."

I exchanged a worried glance with Jenny. Even I knew that

puffer fish preparation was strictly regulated. The toxic parts had to be removed with absolute precision by someone with proper training.

"Excuse me, Nico," I said, stepping forward with a polite but firm smile. "I can't allow you to serve fugu to my guests. The liability issues alone—"

"I trained in Japan for six weeks," Nico interrupted, slamming a knife onto the cutting board with enough force to make us all jump. "And I've done this dozens of times. The video where I prepared fugu got eight million views." He turned to glare at his assistant. "Unlike some people, I actually know what I'm talking about."

"I'm sorry, but this isn't about social media views," I said, crossing my arms. "This is my inn, these are my guests, and I'm responsible for their safety. If something were to happen—"

"Nothing will happen," he said peevishly.

"If it did," I continued firmly, still giving him my steeliest mom stare, "it would be my reputation and my business on the line. Not just yours. No fugu, not here, not tonight."

He stared at me for a long moment, his jaw clenched. I could see the calculations happening behind his eyes. This was a showdown.

"Fine," he finally said with an exaggerated sigh. "I'll use the farm-raised. Happy?"

"Very," I said, relief flooding through me. "Thank you for understanding."

"Whatever," he muttered, turning back to his knives. "I'll make adjustments. The appetizer will still be stunning, just not edgy. Apparently Cypress Grove isn't ready for culinary adventure."

I chose to ignore the barb. "I appreciate your flexibility."

He looked up at me and raised his eyebrow, his mouth in a smirk (one that I'm certain he thought was sexy). It troubled me that he could go from mean as cat poop to sexpot in seconds.

"We'll inform the guests of all ingredients. Then they can

decide whether to eat my food," He waved a dismissive hand. "But don't worry about liability. I have insurance, babycakes." He lifted out what appeared to be a vacuum-sealed package from a container. "Such a shame we can't use this fugu. It's art. The slight tingle of the toxin on the tongue, that's what people pay for. The thrill."

"I'm sure we'll have more than enough thrills without it," I said, though what I really wanted to do was call the health department, and maybe throat punch him. No, that was mean. Violence wouldn't solve anything. But I also knew that canceling the dinner because I was annoyed would disappoint the Chamber of Commerce — and probably result in a lawsuit from this TikTok terror.

He set down the package. "Fine. The *farm-raised* fish will be our first app, to wow everyone at cocktail hour," he continued, now arranging his knives with theatrical precision. "Served as sashimi with a ponzu sauce and gold leaf. Then we move into the dining room with an amuse-bouche of caviar and champagne foam, followed by a local stone crab preparation—"

A crash from the living room cut him off. The three of us peered out. Ben had dropped a box of what looked like tiny glass serving dishes.

"Useless!" Nico shouted, causing his assistant to flinch. "Those were custom made in Venice! Do you know how much they cost?"

"I'm so sorry, Chef, I—"

"Just clean it up. Try not to cut yourself. Actually, no, don't clean it up. You'll probably need stitches if you try." He turned back and gave Jenny a salacious look up and down. I cleared my throat and folded my arms over my chest. Nope, he deserved a throat punch.

"The menu, please," I said in a tone frostier than anticipated.

"Yes." He sighed and ripped his gaze away from my daughter. "We will have, what? Four guests total?"

I counted in my head. "Seven, unless the Chamber adds

people at the last minute. Originally it was six of us, but my daughter..." my voice trailed off and I put my hand on Jenny's arm.

I braced for him to say something nasty because of the addition to the dinner. Instead, he gave a lopsided smile. "Of course Jenny is welcome. I especially love mother-daughter teams."

Jenny turned away, her face red, like she was going to explode with laughter. Me being older and crankier, I simply stared at him, stone faced.

"Too much? Sorry," he said.

"I can contact the Chamber for the latest head count," I said icily.

He shook his head, and it seemed as though he'd dropped his seductive act. "Really, it doesn't matter. I'll make enough for ten, in case there are last minute additions. It'll be no problem, I promise."

"That's good." I tried to put on a tight smile but by now he was ignoring me, focused solely on his knives and the stainless-steel container.

"Influence the influencers," Nico muttered, more to himself than to us. "That's how you build an empire." He began unpacking more equipment, including what looked like a small torch. "Ben! Where are the micro herbs?"

"In the cooler, Chef."

"Well, get them out! They need to come to room temperature." He sighed dramatically. "It's like working with a child. A very slow child."

I'd seen enough. "Jenny, let's check on the dining room again? Make sure everything's perfect?"

My daughter nodded, already backing toward the door. But as we turned to leave, she paused. "Um, Chef Romano?"

"What?" He looked up, annoyed at the interruption.

"I just wanted to say I loved your video about hand-pulled noodles. The one where you talked about your grandmother teaching you? It was really touching."

Something flickered across his face. It seemed like genuine emotion breaking through his carefully crafted persona. But it vanished as quickly as it had appeared.

"Thanks, babe. That video got twelve million views," he said, finally smiling genuinely. "Now, if you'll excuse me, I have a dinner to prepare."

As we walked back to the dining room, Jenny whispered, "Mom, is that fish thing legal?"

I shook my head. "Probably not. But I think he got the message."

"I think so, too. He looked a little afraid of you. But I can't believe he'd risk his career like that." She glanced back toward the kitchen. "Though I guess a trip to the emergency room would definitely get views."

I couldn't help but laugh, even though the situation wasn't funny. "Let's go over the guest list. You can help me figure out where to seat everyone."

We walked back into the dining room, which felt like a tranquil sanctuary compared to the tension swirling in the kitchen. I pulled out my phone where I'd saved the dinner reservations in a notes app and began to explain the guest list to Jenny.

Ben appeared in the doorway with more of Nico's equipment. He paused, watching Jenny. She was hoisting an oversize vase from the sideboard to a smaller table near the window.

"That looks really nice," he said, but looked away when he saw I was listening. "The, um, pineapple, I mean. Can I help? That vase looks heavy."

Jenny smiled. "I've got it, but thanks for wanting to help."

He stayed for a few more moments, then Nico's voice bellowed from the kitchen. Poor Ben. It was clear he wanted to get away from his boss, and I couldn't blame him. But why didn't the guy quit? I guess that working for an influencer or whatever kids called it these days was lucrative. I made a mental shrug while pulling out my phone. I typed a quick message to Kristan.

Just double checking final headcount for tonight. Any last-minute changes I should know about?

The three dots appeared immediately, then disappeared. Then appeared again. I checked a few other texts and snuck a look at the inn's Facebook page, then navigated back to my texts. Why hadn't Kristan gotten back to me? Usually she was on top of every message within seconds.

"Looks like she's typing a novel," Jenny said, peering over my shoulder. She'd run outside and grabbed some of the pink flowers, and was now arranging them around the pineapple centerpiece, making it look even more elegant.

The antique doorbell chimed, a melodic sound that always reminded me of Victorian carolers. My stomach did a flip. "Oh no, please don't let that be the other dinner guests already. I haven't even changed out of these clothes. They can't be two hours early."

I glanced down at my wrinkled cotton dress, which had an unidentified stain. Ugh.

"Want me to get it?" Jenny asked.

Before either of us could move, a woman appeared in the dining room doorway. She was around my age, dressed in crisp white linen shorts and a turquoise T-shirt that managed to look both casual and expensive. Her honey-blonde hair was greasy, though, and looked like she hadn't washed it in a few days.

"Hi, hello?" she called out. "The front desk was empty, so I walked in. I'm so sorry."

Thunder rolled across the sky as I hurried forward. "No, I'm sorry. I'm Amelia Matthews, the owner."

"Clara Whitman." She extended a hand. "The Chamber sent me. They said you'd have a room opening up today, and..." Her eyes swept over the set table in the dining room. "They mentioned you might have space at tonight's dinner? I know it's last minute, but they assured me it wouldn't be a problem."

I blinked, both at her sudden appearance and at a crack of thunder, one that seemed close. A room opening up? I did have one, but usually people didn't stroll in off the street — most folks who frequented B&Bs knew to make reservations in advance. And the dinner was already pushing capacity with the current guest list. How would Nico react if I told him an eighth person was coming?

My phone buzzed. Kristan's message had finally arrived.

Before I could check it, a crash echoed from the kitchen, followed by Nico's voice: "FOR THE LOVE OF GOD, BEN, THOSE WERE IMPORTED FROM ITALY!" He followed that up with a string of swear words that would be more at home in a truck stop.

I winced and looked at Clara, whose mouth dropped open for a brief second. Outside, the first fat drops of rain slapped against the windows. The storm that had threatened all afternoon was finally rolling in. I should make sure the umbrella stand was near the door for the guests.

"That's our visiting chef," I explained weakly. "He's intense about his craft."

"Gotcha." She smiled, then glanced nervously at the pretty dining room table. "I was downtown and intended to stay there longer, but realized I needed to get here before the weather got bad. The radio kept warning about severe storms coming into the area."

I glanced from her to Jenny, then back to Clara. She licked her lips nervously then her words tumbled out.

"I'm so sorry to bust in on you like this, at the last minute. I'm moving from the suburbs of Boston to a small town on the Gulf Coast. Driving, actually. Well, this is my second trip, I brought my dog earlier and he's at my new place. A college friend works at the Chamber here in town. I'm ah, getting a divorce and starting a new life in Florida, over in Sunny Shores. You know, near Tampa?"

I nodded, and as I studied the pretty woman, I saw the overwhelm in her tired eyes. "Yes, I've heard of it. It's famous for its flowers, right?"

She swallowed hard. "Yes, that's the place. My college friend works at the Chamber here, her name's Kristan. She suggested I stop in, and said I might want to check out tonight's pop up and the town for a night or two. I'm doing something similar, a pop-up. Well, I'm actually running a flower truck, but I want to do pop-ups. Or will be, once I get to Sunny Shores. Sorry, I'm babbling. My life's a little out of control right now. Anyway, my friend said the women here in town have a special bond. Special powers. I wanted to see what that was like. Apparently there are a few towns like this in Florida, and Sunny Shores is one, and..."

Her voice trailed off, and the full picture was beginning to emerge. So Kristan was her friend and referred her here. Okay, this all made more sense now.

Clara's voice had that slightly manic edge I remembered from my own early post-divorce days. That need to explain everything at once, as if you had to justify your entire existence to strangers. I'd done the same thing, watching people's faces for judgment or pity.

"You don't need to apologize," I said softly. "I get it. I went through my own divorce a few years ago." I gestured around the inn. "This place was my fresh start."

Some of the tension left Clara's shoulders and suddenly, I wanted to make sure this woman had a fun night to take her mind off her troubles. "Really?"

"Really. And as it happens, I do have a room available. Someone checked out this morning." I didn't mention that I'd been planning to move some furniture around in there before the next guest arrived in a few days. That could wait. "And I'm sure we can squeeze in one more for dinner. I'm happy to have you. This will be a fun little trip for you. You're going to love Cypress Grove."

From the kitchen came the sound of Nico shouting about proper knife technique, followed by Ben's stammered apology.

Clara gave a nervous laugh. "Are you sure? It sounds like someone in there is already stressed out, maybe more than me."

"Oh, he's, you know..." I waved my hand dismissively. "Being a chef. Trust me, you'll want to be here for this dinner. It's going to be memorable." *One way or another*, I thought, but didn't say it out loud.

Jenny stepped forward. "Mom makes everyone feel welcome," she said, and something in her voice made me turn to look at her. She was watching me with an expression I hadn't seen in a while. Maybe ever. It was a mix of pride and understanding that made my heart squeeze. "It's kind of her superpower."

I swallowed past the sudden lump in my throat. "Thank you, honey," I murmured, then turned to Clara. "This is my daughter, Jenny. Come on, I'll show you to your room. We can get you settled in before the dinner begins."

"I can grab fresh towels if you tell me where they are," Jenny offered. "And if you'd like, I have a couple extra sheet masks for your face, if you want to chill out in your room for a while."

I snapped my fingers and grinned. "Great idea, Jen. I could send up a bottle of wine, too."

Clara blinked rapidly. "You're both so kind. I wasn't expecting this." She took a deep breath and looked like she might burst into tears. "My friend said this town was special, but I thought she was referring to the psychic stuff."

"Oh, it's definitely that too," I said with a laugh. "But this, Florida, is a place where people can reinvent themselves. Trust me, I know." I picked up one of her bags. "The room has a lovely view of the garden, and there's a coffee shop downtown that makes the best iced lavender honey lattes you've ever tasted."

"Plus," Jenny added, "if you're into flowers, you should see what Mom's employee Jimbo has done with the herb garden. He's some kind of plant whisperer."

I shot Jenny a surprised look. Wasn't she the one who'd been rolling her eyes about Jimbo's plant shaman abilities earlier? She shrugged and gave me a small smile.

"Let me check this message real quick," I said, pulling out my phone.

> Hey, it's Kristan! Sending someone your way! Clara W, friend of mine from college. She needs the Crescent Moon magic. Can you work some of your special hospitality? Will explain more later. Adding her to dinner list, I'll tell Nico. Sorry for last minute!! I'll see all y'all for dinner soon.

I smiled. "Well, looks like the universe knew what it was doing. Welcome to Cypress Grove, Clara. I think you're going to fit right in."

Seven

I picked up one of Clara's bags, a tattered brown leather duffel that had definitely seen better days, and led her up the grand staircase. "The room has some quirks, as does everything in this town," I said, noting how she trailed her fingers along the mahogany bannister, much as I had done my first day here. "But I suspect you'll love it."

Room 203 was one of my favorites, and the one I first stayed in when I arrived here nine months ago. It had a large bank of windows overlooking the backyard garden. A golden loveseat and matching chair was on one side of the room, and I'd added some new touches to the gold, lilac, and cream décor — namely some shelves with delicate glass bottles, filled with fresh, faintly purple roses. Next to them sat various trinkets I'd picked up at local antique stores. Tiny spell books, porcelain teacups, and some candles.

Those were battery-powered, since I didn't trust any guest with open flames. I'd learned that the hard way the first month I was here, when four women who were my age attempted to contact Kurt Cobain, the singer of Nirvana, during a séance. Fortunately, I'd been in the hall and smelled smoke, and only the edge of a curtain had been set ablaze.

Today, the late afternoon light filtered through lace curtains, catching dust in its wake. Ugh. I silently winced. It was as if I could never clean enough to get rid of the dust. Then again, I liked to think of the stuff as magical sprinkles, infusing the guests with a relaxed, happy vibe. Yeah. Magic pixie dust. That was the ticket.

"Oh, how beautiful!" Clara's eyes lit up as she spotted a squat bookcase. She tilted her head sideways, reading the spines. "Are these mysteries?"

"Yes. I've shuffled some things around since inheriting the inn, and felt these looked nice in here." I watched as she examined the books. "My aunt collected them. Everything from vintage Agatha Christie to modern true crime. I've added a few of my own, as well."

"'The Poisoner's Handbook,'" Clara read aloud, pulling out a well-worn volume. "'Lady Killers,' 'Death in the Garden.'" She turned to me with a sparkle in her eye that transformed her entire face. "I love true crime and stuff like this. My dad, he's a detective back in Boston. He used to hate that I listened to murder podcasts while arranging flowers at my old shop."

I leaned against the doorway, wondering whether to mention my own involvement in solving local murders. Clara seemed like a woman who would be interested in that sort of thing. Then again, given Jenny's earlier reaction to my psychometric abilities, maybe it was best to keep that particular detail to myself. At least for the moment.

Clara returned the book and selected another. "My ex never understood my fascination, either. He and my dad work in the same precinct, actually. They both thought it was weird that I wanted to be a crime scene tech before..." She trailed off, her fingers caressing the book's spine.

"Before?" I prompted gently.

"Before I got married young and opened a flower shop instead." She shrugged it off, but I detected the hint of old hurt in her voice. "That was more 'appropriate' for a cop's wife, apparently. I wish I had guts back then like I do now."

She gave a brittle laugh.

"We all wish we could have a do-over," I said, thinking of my own ex-husband and how I'd gone into marriage blindly. "Then again, all of our experiences brought us to this moment, and this is a pretty good moment, isn't it?"

She beamed. "It sure the heck is."

I watched as she wandered to the window and inspected a potted plant. It was one of Jimbo's special fern crossbreeds. Her hand reached out as if drawn to it.

"This feels different," she murmured, then stopped herself and hesitated for a second. "Sorry, that probably sounds strange. I've always had a thing with plants and flowers. Like they talk to me, almost?" She laughed nervously. "And I sound completely crazy now. Don't mind me. I'm sure it's divorce or menopause or midlife."

Or perhaps not. Not in Cypress Grove.

"Trust me." I thought of my own journey of discovery in town. "You don't sound crazy at all. I've heard way weirder. You don't even rate on the weird-o-meter."

Laughing, she moved to set her bag down, but her eyes kept darting back to the bookcase. "I probably shouldn't admit this, given everything, but I've been binge-listening to this true crime podcast about poisonous plants on my drive down. The things people can do with everyday flowers." She shook her head. "Sorry. You're going to think I'm a weirdo and kick me out."

I had to laugh. If she only knew about the ghost I'd helped cross over, or the elderly, undead baker who'd showed up in my living room a few months back. "In this town, that's practically small talk. Though maybe we shouldn't mention poisonous plants at dinner tonight. Our chef might take offense, thinking you're trying to steal his thunder or something."

We both giggled. Clara relaxed visibly at my joke, sinking onto the loveseat. "Thanks for this. When Kristan suggested I stop here, I wasn't sure. Didn't want to impose. But there's something about this place." She gestured vaguely at the room, the books, the plant. "It feels right. Like I was meant to be here."

I knew that feeling all too well. How many of us had been called to magical places over the years? I thought about telling her then, about my psychometry, how this town had awakened something in me I hadn't known existed. But the memory of Jenny's skepticism was still too fresh.

"Can I tell you something?" Clara asked, her fingers tracing the edge of the loveseat. "You seem like someone who'd understand."

"Of course." I settled into the matching chair, recognizing the expression of a woman who needed to talk. This came with the territory of being an innkeeper, and I took that part of the job seriously.

"I was married for twenty-five years. We tried to have kids for most of them." She gave a soft laugh, but I heard the hurt beneath it. "Spent a fortune on fertility treatments. Finally came to terms with being childfree, found peace with it. Even started planning cruises to the Caribbean." She shuddered in a breath. "That's when Tom — my ex — announced he was leaving me for a rookie cop. She's thirty."

My heart ached for her. I couldn't imagine navigating both infertility and betrayal. "My ex left me for his secretary. Well, our secretary. It was our business." I kept my voice gentle, not wanting to center my own story.

"No." Clara's lips pulled back into a wince

"Yeah." I didn't get into how the business had been my idea, my baby. Some wounds were still tender.

Clara nodded, then took a deep breath. "Tom's about to be a father. At fifty." She pressed her lips into a thin line. "When he told me, I bought the flower truck that afternoon. Didn't even negotiate the price. Just handed over my credit card and said 'wrap it up, I'm headed to Florida. I'm done with all this crap.'"

"That took courage," I said softly.

"Is it weird that I'm happy for them? Thankful it's not me? And furious? And terrified about starting over?" She gestured at the room. "And also excited?"

"That sounds exactly right." I leaned forward. "My divorce threw me for a loop too. But look at us now — you with your flower truck adventures ahead, me with my inn."

Clara's laugh was genuine this time. "I never expected at forty-eight to be starting over. But you know what? I'm done living in the past. Florida is my fresh start."

"I'm glad it is. Welcome to your new life."

We smiled at each other.

"Well, I should let you get back to the inn," she said.

I stood and she did too. A hug seemed appropriate and I leaned in and embraced her. I could feel the hurt, the confusion, and the hope, coming off her in waves. If anyone needed a hug, it was her.

"Maybe after dinner, over wine, we'll chat more," I said. Once everything downstairs calmed down.

"I'd like that."

As I made my way to the door, I smiled. "Take some time to decompress before cocktails and dinner. The bathroom's stocked with soaps and lotions. Oh, and a shower cap, too. I'll have Jenny bring up the sheet masks and a bottle of wine. Red, white, or bubbly?"

Eight

I left Clara to settle in, grateful for a moment to catch my breath before the next round of chaos began.

The entire event had seemed manageable when the Chamber first proposed it. Now that I was going over the guest list in my mind, however, doubts were setting in. There was Mitzi Blackwood, who never missed a chance to remind everyone she was the longest-serving member of the Cypress Grove City Council.

Then the honeymooning Andersons, who had been at the inn off and on for a few weeks now as they traveled around Florida. They were sweet but oddly fascinated by the inn's spookier aspects. One morning I'd heard a noise in the attic, and had found Marc poking around with a flashlight.

Another guest was my friend Adam Stone, the owner of Grape Escape, who'd specifically requested a seat when he heard about the pop-up dinner series.

Plus Kristan from the Chamber, who'd orchestrated this whole thing.

Now I had two unexpected additions: Jenny, who was still processing the whole witch situation, and Clara, who was running from a failed marriage. At least the dining room was ready, thanks to Jenny's impromptu tablescaping skills. It was a good crowd, right? Individually, everyone was lovely.

But as a professional hostess, I wasn't so certain now, especially with Nico and his skittish assistant in the mix.

I was halfway down the stairs when I heard a ruckus in the kitchen, followed by cursing. What had I gotten myself into, letting a TikTok chef take over my kitchen? The Chamber had assured me that all the visiting chefs were rising stars, but something about him set my teeth on edge. Maybe it was the way he flirted with me *and* Jenny.

A crash from the kitchen made me jump. Nico shouted something about his "process" and "artistic vision." I closed my eyes and took a deep breath, channeling my inner innkeeper Zen. I'd taken a couple of classes at the coven house on meditation techniques, but right now what I really needed was a glass of wine.

Or maybe a protection spell. Yes. That was the ticket. I was learning how to do those, and they were proving surprisingly difficult. Even though my psychometry abilities were strong, my other powers needed a ton of work. That was normal, my coven friends kept assuring me.

Still I had faced down angry ghosts, solved murders, and had divorced the biggest jerk in California. Surely I could handle one temperamental chef.

Another crash. More swearing. Ugh.

Then again, maybe I should text Oliver. He had a way of diffusing tense situations, and—

No. I could handle this myself. Besides, now that Jenny was here, I needed to be mindful of how she'd react to his presence. It was anyone's guess at this point. In my mind, I imagined taking both of them out for brunch, sitting somewhere neutral on a Sunday morning and having a warm, happy chat.

Sunday was days away.

But perhaps I could use some of my new spell knowledge to help smooth over this sticky situation tonight. I ducked into the library and went to the roll-top desk that was mostly for decoration. It was where I kept a small pouch of herbs, and I took out a small, burlap bag. The soothing scent of lavender wafted to my nose, and I inhaled. The calming scent instantly made me feel a little better.

I'd chosen the ingredients carefully: lavender for peace, rosemary for protection, and a pinch of sage that Jimbo had grown specifically for banishing negative energy. Mixed with a few other herbs from my garden, it was a blend my friend Renee swore by for creating a sphere of safety.

Protection spells were particularly tricky, I had learned. One had to maintain absolute focus while reciting the words correctly. The herbs needed to form a perfect circle, and the intent had to be pure. No anger, no fear. Only the clear desire to create a safe space.

Focus was in short supply today, at least in this place. I imagined Renee's voice: "The spell works even when you think it hasn't. Magic has its own timing."

I sprinkled the herbs in a tight circle around me, making sure to create an unbroken line. The lavender and sage released more of their aromatic oils as they hit the floor. I closed my eyes and began Renee's go-to incantation. "By earth and air, by fire and sea—"

"What are you doing?"

I jumped, scattering herbs everywhere. The floor looked like the night Freddie had clawed his way into a bag of organic catnip.

Nico stood in the doorway, shirtless, looking at me like I'd lost my mind. Which, to be fair, probably appeared to be the case. Then again, he was half naked in a stranger's home, so who was the eccentric one here? Why was he shirtless?

"I was, you know." I scrambled to sweep the herbs under the desk with my foot. A dust bunny joined the party, making me feel even more unprepared for this entire evening. Where had that come from? "Tidying up."

"With your eyes closed?" One of his perfectly sculpted eyebrows lifted. "While chanting? Or was it a love spell?"

He grinned.

"Of course it wasn't a love spell," I said a little too sharply. "It's a meditation technique. For stress management."

I felt my face growing hot. Even after all these months in Cypress Grove, I still wasn't used to practicing magic in front of anyone outside of the coven and my close friends, much less skeptics. Especially not judgmental, shirtless skeptics who smelled like a combination of fish and way too much cologne. Plus the threat of poisonous fish. Sheesh!

Duck this guy. I stared at him sourly, unblinking.

He rolled his eyes, obviously giving up the charade of flirtation. "This town. This whole state. Meh. No wonder the food scene is stuck in the dark ages. I can't wait to get to Los Angeles."

He turned on his heel and strode out, his back muscles rippling. I was left standing there with scattered herbs and a half-finished protection spell that definitely wasn't going to work now.

I reached for my special jar of consecrated sea salt to attempt another spell. Liz had helped me charge the salt under the full moon. I normally kept it in one of the desk drawers, but my hand met empty air. Frowning, I checked the other shelves and the drawers. Where had I put it? I could have sworn it was right here with my other ritual supplies.

"Jenny?" I called out.

"Mom?" She bustled into the room.

"Did you move any jars or items in this desk while you were decorating?"

"No. Only the centerpiece and linens. I hadn't even noticed this was here. Cool old piece, though."

"Okay, thanks. Never mind then."

She shrugged. "I'm grabbing some more flowers from the garden."

As she walked out, I massaged the back of my neck. Some of the older women in the coven mentioned this, how once perimenopause was in full swing, the brain fog took over. Was that happening now?

Oh well. The salt would turn up eventually. I went to the hall closet, found a broom and dustpan, then gave the library floor a good sweep. Though as I worked, I noticed something odd. The herbs seemed to resist being gathered up, as if they wanted to stay where they'd fallen. Even the dustpan felt unusually heavy. I shook the contents into the small garbage can near the desk, figuring that they'd at least make the room smell nice.

I was almost finished when I heard the front door burst open. The Andersons tumbled into the library, their faces pink with excitement. Or sunstroke. Hard to tell here in Florida. I stashed the broom and dustpan back into the closet.

Sarah's short hair was windswept, and Marc's polo shirt had mysterious dirt stains on the sleeves.

"Amelia!" Sarah called out, clutching her husband's arm. "You'll never believe what happened on our ghost tour!"

I paused in the foyer, hearing what sounded like pots banging together from the kitchen. That had better be his cookware. If Nico ruined even one piece of my All-Clad, we were going to come to blows.

I scratched my neck. "Oh?"

"We saw an actual spirit!" Marc's eyes were wide behind his wire-rimmed glasses. "At the old theater downtown! Our EMF meter went crazy, and then—"

"BEN!" Nico's bellow cut through their story. "WHERE IS THE MOLECULAR GASTRONOMY KIT?"

I forced a tight smile and pretended I hadn't heard Nico. "That's wonderful about the ghost. Why don't you two get ready for dinner? We're starting soon. We're planning on having cocktails first in the library downstairs. You know where that is, right? Of course you do."

Nodding, they hurried upstairs, still chattering about orbs and energy readings. I hadn't had the heart to tell them that the theater ghost was actually just Bill, a retired citrus grower who liked to mess with tourists by wearing a sheet and making spooky noises. The local ghost tour guides were in on the joke.

There were many real ghosts in Cypress Grove, but Bill wasn't among them.

Then again, it was entirely possible they had detected something else. Who knew? I didn't have time to ponder because by now, it was perilously close to cocktail hour and this weird dinner. The pufferfish dish still had me on edge. Nico had me on edge.

The entire vibe was off.

<h1 style="text-align:center">Nine</h1>

The next hour passed in a blur of last-minute cleaning.

Mitzi Blackwood arrived first, wearing a designer dress that probably cost more than my college education. She paused mid-air-kiss as a brief flash of lightning flickered through the front windows. "Oh dear, that storm's getting close. The weather alert on my phone said we might see flooding tonight." She touched her designer dress. "I do hope everyone can make it home safely after dinner."

"I'm sure it will blow over," I said. Mitzi flitted away, declaring that she wanted to inspect the patterned Victorian wallpaper in the parlor. She'd known my late aunt, and I told her to make herself at home.

Fifteen minutes later, Adam from Grape Escape arrived. He was damp from the light rain that had started, and carrying a beautiful bouquet of stunning, deep purple carnations, and a canvas bag filled with wine. He set down the wine bottles and handed me the flowers, while water dripped from his jacket onto my hardwood floors.

"Thank you," I cooed. "They're beautiful."

"Sorry about the mess. It's about to come down out there." He shucked off his jacket and I reached for it. "Weather service says it's going to get worse before it gets better. One of those slow-moving systems."

"Oh no," I groaned. That probably meant people would linger. Something I'd noticed about Floridians was that they treated rain like folks in the north handled snow: they tended to hunker, as if water would make them dissolve.

"Yeah. I'm worried about Paulie. This is his first big storm." Adam and his boyfriend had recently adopted a twelve-week-old Husky puppy.

"Oof. I hope you have a Thundershirt ready. Is Jason with him?"

Adam nodded.

I suggested Adam bring his wine to the library, and scurried away to put his jacket in a closet and to find a vase for the bouquet in the downstairs bathroom off the lobby. Clara appeared, looking a tad nervous, as if she wasn't sure she belonged here.

"Hey there," I called out from the bathroom. "How are you feeling?"

"Much better. That Pinot was delicious. I only had a glass but I suspect I'll have more later."

"That's the spirit," I said in a hearty tone.

I emerged from the bathroom, holding the vase. Clara had changed into an understated but elegant cocktail dress that went well with her pale, freckled New England roots: a loose navy cotton jersey dress with three-quarter length sleeves and a swing skirt. It sported a subtle boat neckline that suggested quiet sophistication. She wore nude sandals, and delicate pearl earrings that looked like they might have been a family heirloom.

A thin silver bracelet, simple and classic, circled her wrist. Her hair was pulled back in a neat, low chignon that screamed practicality and restraint. She was effortlessly elegant, which made me a little envious.

"Well, I'm glad. You look gorgeous," I said, setting the flowers on the front desk. She grinned, and I was happy that I'd at least made someone's night a little brighter. Because I had my doubts whether our chef would come away pleased from this evening, and I wasn't looking forward to *that* blowback.

Clara and I gushed over the bouquet, and she told me about her flower truck business, which sounded like something we could use here in Cypress Grove.

Moments later, Kristan Jones swept in, her arms full of promotional materials about our town's culinary scene. She hugged Clara warmly, and I caught fragments of their whispered conversation about "new beginnings" and "fresh starts," and how Clara's ex-husband, a cop in Massachusetts, was, by Kristan's estimation, "a pimple on the butt of progress."

I stifled a snicker at that.

Leaving them in the lobby, I figured this was the best time to escape into my apartment to change. In my bedroom, which was still awash in Jenny's belongings, I pulled out my favorite dress: a flowing, light cotton sapphire number with bell sleeves and subtle silver embroidery around the hem and neckline. A member of my coven had actually enchanted the fabric to stay cool in summer heat.

Freddie lazed on the bed, deep into his seventeenth hour of napping. He rolled onto his back. I leaned over to grab his ample, soft belly. "I want to be you, mister cat man," I said in a growly voice.

"Mom?" Jenny appeared in the doorway. "Is that what you're wearing?"

"Yes?" I straightened to sit and smoothed the soft fabric. "What's wrong with it?"

"Nothing, it's just. Um." She gestured, waggling her fingers in my direction. "Very. Witchy."

I chuckled. "And?"

"It's so different from the things you used to wear in California."

"True." I moved to the dresser, where I extracted a ruby pendant that my aunt had left for me. I fastened it around my neck. I wasn't afraid of clashing colors these days.

"You used to wear Land's End and LL Bean, and what was that other brand?"

It was true. For Jenny's entire life, we'd lived in the heart of wine country, and my style had been both preppy and practical. Also deathly dull. "Talbot's. I was so sad when they closed that store in Napa."

"Yeah, but this, your new style, it's so unusual. You look less like a mom and more like, I dunno. A crone-to-be. Or like Stevie Nicks without the white parrot."

I grinned. "Good." I had to admit the silver symbols embroidered along the neckline weren't exactly subtle. But who cared? Not me. "Besides, this is Cypress Grove. Everyone expects a little offbeat attire."

"The city council lady looks like she's wearing Chanel," Jenny pointed out.

"Well, I'm wearing enchanted organic cotton, and it's going to keep me comfortable. As you get older, you'll realize that breathable fabric is the best thing since sliced bread." I twisted my hair up into a messy ponytail-slash-bun, secured it with a decorative stick carved with protection runes (a coven sister sold those at street fairs), and added my favorite red lipstick. I smacked my mouth and stuffed my feet into a pair of white Birkenstock sandals.

"Listen," I said. "Is Nico bothering you? Being inappropriate? Because if he is—"

"No, Mom. He hasn't said a word to me at all. Thank God. I think he's creepy."

"I do, too. If he does anything inappropriate, he's going to have me to deal with, and I'll send him and his pufferfish packing in the rain."

"Okay, settle down, Mom. You look great. Weird, but great. I'm going to check on the table one last time." She hurried out.

I smiled at my image in the mirror. The entire bathroom, including the shelf near the antique claw foot tub, was now surrounded by a dizzying array of my daughter's bathing products. I suspected my ex had given her a nearly unlimited credit card to Sephora.

As I was about to leave to face the chaos of the dinner, a thought popped into my head.

Settling onto the edge of the tub, I pulled my phone out of my purse. If I was going to host this chef and keep the conversation flowing tonight, I should probably see what all the fuss was about. Jenny had mentioned TikTok, and while I usually avoided social media like a curse (pun intended), this seemed like necessary research.

"Okay, Interwebs," I muttered. "How do I find someone on TikTok?"

Ten minutes and several accidental swipes later, I found Nico's profile. His handle was @ChefJAfterDark, which seemed a bit ridiculous. Then again, everything on TikTok seemed ridiculous.

The first video that popped up showed him aggressively kneading bread dough while wearing a tank top that had to be at least two sizes too small. The caption read "Sometimes you gotta show that dough who's boss." He slapped the dough lasciviously, and I briefly shut my eyes. Gah. Jenny hadn't been joking.

Was this what younger women had to deal with?

I cringed but kept scrolling. In the next video, he was telling a supposedly heartwarming story about learning to make noodles from his grandmother, but something felt off. The timing was too perfect, the emotion too practiced. My psychometry might not work through phone screens, but my middle-aged BS detector was pinging like crazy.

Then I found something interesting. Another chef had "dueted" one of Nico's videos (Jenny would have to explain that term to me later). This chef, an older woman with grey hair and serious eyes, was pointing out all the ways Nico's sushi preparation went against all Japanese norms.

"This man is appropriating culture," she said firmly.

The comments section was even more revealing. Former

employees sharing stories of corners cut, ingredients mishandled, people getting sick. One comment stuck out: "Remember Tampa? He's lucky that health inspector took early retirement instead of pressing charges."

Yikes. Why had the Chamber invited this guy?

I was so absorbed that I almost forgot about the time. A clang from somewhere in the inn snapped me back to the present. Right. I had an event here, whether I liked this chef or not. It was my responsibility to get everyone through the night without incident or illness.

But as I reapplied my lipstick (my signature shade, which was supposed to last through anything but never quite did), I couldn't shake an uneasy feeling. Something about Nico wasn't merely obnoxious. It was ominous.

Then again, maybe I was being paranoid. Not everything in Cypress Grove had to be spooky or strange. I'd simply keep an eye on the food and put my foot down if something seemed wildly out of place.

When I emerged from my bedroom, I walked down the hall and paused at the kitchen doorway. What I saw made me want to gasp. Or snort.

Nico was performing for Ben's camera setup, which involved three iPhones on an elaborate telescoping mount. Nico slowly licked the edge of a knife while gazing smolderingly into the lens.

Eww. Eww. Eww. Did anyone actually think this was sexy? Was this what the younger generation liked? Did Jenny find this attractive? Whatever happened to the art of subtle flirtation? My mind spun with plans for a heart-to-heart with her. I didn't want her to waste one moment of her precious life on men like this. Regardless of how many social media followers he had.

I kept watching the absurd scene. Nico set the knife down and stared at Ben and his camera. He dipped his thumb into a bowl filled with a green, frothy substance. Wasabi, perhaps?

Then he licked his thumb slowly, waggling his tongue. I nearly gagged.

"Things are about to get hot," he said in a sultry voice. "And I'm not just talking about the stove."

Oh come on, dude. I rolled my eyes. *Barf.*

"CUT! Perfect, Chef!" Ben adjusted something on one of the phones. "The lighting is catching the blade beautifully."

A brilliant flash of lightning illuminated the kitchen, followed immediately by a deafening crack of thunder that made Ben jump and almost drop his phone setup. The lights flickered.

"If we lose power, I swear to—" Nico began, but I stepped forward and cut him off.

"The inn has a generator," I firmly assured him, though I wasn't entirely sure how it worked, if we had enough gas, or if it would even last longer than a few minutes. The notes Aunt Shirley had left behind about the backup electric system had been cryptic at best (and also involved a spell).

Ben stammered. Nico scowled. I scowled harder. His olive complexion gleamed with sweat (or perhaps body oil) and he flexed his pectorals. Or maybe he was having some weird muscle spasm.

"Fine," he finally said.

Nodding, I walked out, thanking the universe that I wasn't a regular on TikTok, otherwise I'd probably be banned for making some snarky Gen X-flavored comments.

The library, which was right outside my apartment door, was where we were doing the cocktail hour prior to dinner. I probably should have decorated the space, but it was funky and gothic enough to keep everyone engaged. I hoped.

Jenny bustled in. When she'd had time to change into a cute, black cotton dress and sandals was a mystery. I spotted a familiar turquoise amulet around her neck.

"Is that my necklace?"

She nodded. "I found it in your jewelry box. Hope that's okay. Can I help with drinks? I know how to make basic cocktails from that catering gig."

"Thanks, honey, but—" I broke off as Nico's voice boomed from the kitchen.

"BEN! We need another angle on this knife work. The followers need to FEEL the danger! And no man titty!"

Jenny and I met each other's eyes. "I'm not even going to ask," I said.

"Mom, there are a lot of people milling around the lobby and the dining room and that other weird room."

"What other weird room? The one with the TV or the one with the Wiccan altar?"

"Uh, I guess the altar."

"That's the parlor."

"Want me to bring them in here? Or the dining room?"

I chewed on my cheek. My initial plan was to have casual cocktails, then we'd move to the dining room. But since Nico was closer to the library than the dining room — and since he was having a tantrum every five minutes — perhaps the guests should be kept elsewhere. Then again, I didn't want them to ruin the table spread prior to dinner. Something told me Nico wouldn't appreciate that for his video.

"Let's bring them in the library, in here." My gaze swept over the leather chairs and sofa. This was such a cozy, sumptuous space, perfect for a pre-dinner glass of wine. "We've got plenty of room."

I glanced at my phone, tempted to text Oliver despite my reservations. He was excellent in chaotic situations. But no, he had plans with his musician friends tonight and I didn't want to interrupt.

"Mom?" Jenny's voice pulled me back. "Where do you keep the ice?"

"Oh, right. It's in the—" I turned to point her toward the vintage ice bucket, but Mitzi Blackwood appeared at my elbow. The guests weren't waiting to be invited in.

"Amelia, darling," she drawled, "I simply must know where

you found this marvelous grandfather clock. My husband and I are redecorating our foyer."

Before I could answer, Adam wandered past, heading toward the kitchen. "Just going to check on things," he called out, his tone oddly tight.

"Wait—" I started after him, suspecting that Nico wouldn't want to be interrupted while he was filming his shirtless schtick, or whatever he was doing. Also, I was in charge of the wine. But Adam didn't listen, and he went through the bookcase door and into my apartment. I was beyond caring at this point.

I turned back to Jenny. "Let's arrange the wine glasses on that tray."

I noticed Ben hovering nearby, offering to carry the tray for my daughter. His eagerness to help would have been sweet under different circumstances. Unlike Nico's obvious leering, Ben's attention seemed almost protective, if a bit awkward.

"What are YOU doing in here?" Nico's voice wafted from the kitchen. "I don't need your amateur wine suggestions!"

"Amateur?" The other man's laugh was Adam's. How did he know Nico? "That's rich, coming from someone who wouldn't know a Bordeaux from a box wine before I—" He lowered his voice and I couldn't hear the rest.

Goodness. Should I intervene? What was going on? Maybe the Florida culinary scene was smaller than I thought. Whatever. I needed to gather everyone for drinks. Nico and Adam could sort it out on their own. Or not. They were grown men.

I hustled into the foyer to find the Andersons taking selfies with Georgina the alligator.

"Wine's ready in the library," I said. "Oh, and have you seen Kristan and Clara?"

The two looked up from their phones. "I don't know who they are," Sarah said. "Sorry."

"No worries." I scooted back to the library, where Jenny was filling an ice bucket.

"Found it in that weird cabinet with all the crystals. Also, I think someone went upstairs? I heard footsteps."

Perfect. My guests were wandering all over the inn, Nico was one criticism away from a meltdown, and I couldn't keep track of anyone. From the kitchen came the distinct sound of Ben's heavy sigh, followed by more arguing.

"I need to check on that situation," I said, aiming for the kitchen. "Jenny, could you attempt to corral everyone?"

"Sure, Mom. I'll tell them I know something about seances."

I hurried toward the kitchen, cursing the Chamber of Commerce for this entire idea. The evening hadn't even started, and already it felt like a disaster. All I wanted was to take my daughter out for a nice chicken parm sandwich (her favorite) and continue talking.

"Can I do anything to help?" Kristan asked, appearing at my elbow.

"Oh!" Her sudden presence startled me. "Well, if you could greet everyone, that would be amazing. I'm a little behind on a few things."

"Of course, sweetie." She beamed.

I squeezed her arm and whispered thanks. I didn't know Kristan well, but from the little I did, I knew she was efficient and hyper-organized, always toting both an iPad and a paper planner around.

Tonight she wore a cream-colored jumpsuit that somehow managed to look both professional and bohemian, offset by a chunky gold necklace. Her chestnut-hued hair was a contrast to her peachy complexion. It was twisted into one of those artfully messy buns that took an hour to look effortlessly undone. Similar to my daughter's, in fact.

When had everyone learned to do their hair like that? Whenever I tried to sweep my hair up, I looked like I'd tried and failed to flee a tornado.

Everything about Kristan was like that: carefully curated to appear casual. She'd mentioned that she'd moved to Cypress

Grove about two years ago, but she already seemed intertwined in the community's fabric.

According to others around town, she'd rapidly become indispensable at the Chamber, the kind of person who knew everyone and smoothed every ruffled feather with such practiced ease that you hardly noticed her doing it. Even now, she was greeting guests with the precise movements of someone who'd done it thousands of times before, even though I don't think she'd ever set foot into the Crescent Moon.

Before I went into my apartment, I made eye contact with Kristan again. She flashed another warm smile. That eased my fears a little. I had help.

I found Adam and Nico facing off in my kitchen. The tension in the air was thick, as if Gordon Ramsay had a showdown with the Real Housewives.

Adam's normally cheerful, cute face was flushed with anger, while Nico stood — still inexplicably shirtless, which made me wonder if he was going to serve dinner that way — by my butcher block, a set of extremely sharp knives laid out before him. Ben was huddled in the corner with his phone setup, looking like he wanted to melt into the wall.

That makes two of us, dude, I wanted to say.

"You're a fraud," Adam was saying, his voice tight. "You learned everything you know about wine from me, and now you're going to stand there and reject my selections?"

I glanced between them, confused. "Hold on. Do you two know each other? Nico, I thought you were from Miami."

"Oh, he's from Miami now?" Adam's laugh was bitter. "That's rich. Tell her about Tampa, Nico. Tell her about who gave you your first sommelier job."

"Ancient history," Nico sneered, picking up one of his knives. The blade caught the light as he turned it. "Your pedestrian palate might have been fine for my early career, but I've evolved. My followers expect excellence."

I cleared my throat. "Gentlemen—"

"Stay out of this," Nico snapped, not even looking at me. He began arranging thin slices of what I assumed was the fugu on a crystal plate I definitely hadn't provided. "Ben! Are you getting this? The lighting needs to be perfect."

"Yes, Chef," Ben mumbled, adjusting something on his elaborate phone mount.

I ran a hand over my forehead. Things were spinning out of control.

Adam let out another harsh laugh. "You can't even plate fish without filming it? This is what's wrong with cooking today. All show, no substance."

Jenny appeared at my elbow and murmured into my ear while flashing me her phone. "Mom? The weather radar looks really bad. Like, scary bad." The app displayed an angry mass of red and purple over the entirety of Cypress Grove. "The roads around the inn..."

"Might be flooding," I finished for her.

She nodded grimly and wandered off.

Meanwhile, Nico was glaring at Adam. "Two million views say otherwise," Nico told him. He paused his plating to take a sip from a smoking cocktail glass that definitely hadn't come from my kitchen. The liquid inside was an unnaturally bright blue and appeared to be glowing.

Erm. What was in that, anyway? Probably blue curacao liquor and a fancy smoker device, if I had to guess.

"Now, if you'll excuse me, I have guests to dazzle," Nico said.

It was then that I realized he'd changed into tight leather pants with a wide, round silver belt buckle, and black leather biker boots. He was still shirtless. This was turning into a farce.

He grabbed both the cocktail and a stainless steel plate that held some minimalist dish, then shouldered past me into the library. Adam and I exchanged looks.

"I'm sorry," I said softly. "I had no idea he'd be like this. Or that you knew him. I'm honestly baffled by everything."

Adam's expression softened. "Not your fault, Amelia. But

that man, ugh." He shook his head. "Let's just say there's a reason he's not welcome in most professional kitchens in Tampa anymore. Or anywhere, for that matter."

Before I could ask what he meant, we heard Nico's voice boom from the library: "Ladies and gentlemen! Prepare yourselves for a culinary experience that will revolutionize the sleepy food scene of this charming little village."

The way he said "village" made it sound like a slur.

"Yikes, yikes, yikes," I muttered, hurrying toward the library with Adam close behind. Ben scurried after us, his camera rig held high to capture whatever was about to unfold.

Ten

I rushed into the library right in time to see my guests' reactions.

Mitzi Blackwood's perfectly plucked eyebrows shot up so high they nearly disappeared into her hairline. The Andersons gaped, while Clara seemed to be studying her shoes with intense fascination. That poor woman probably thought this would be an elegant and classy event.

Jenny, bless her, was holding a tray of glasses half filled with white wine. I knew from her expression that she was also stifling a belly laugh.

Nico took a dramatic sip of his blue cocktail, then gestured at Ben to make sure he was filming. "You see this drink? I call it 'Electric Dreams.' Molecular gastronomy meets mixology meets..." He paused for effect. "Performance art."

The Andersons applauded politely. Mitzi beamed and eyed his six-pack stomach. Nico winked at her saucily.

Cringe, as the kids would say.

"And this," he held up the plate of fish, "this is what separates the artists from the amateurs. Real fugu, prepared by a master." He smirked at Adam. "Not some small town wine bar yokel who thinks visiting Italy twice makes him an expert."

Adam snorted audibly.

Ben positioned himself in the corner, cameras ready. The whole scene felt surreal: the gothic library with its leather-bound books and crystal balls serving as backdrop to this half-naked TikTok chef's grandiose performance. I sagged against the side of a bookcase in the back of the room, mortified.

Questions raced through my mind as I stared at the bizarro situation.

Had Adam intentionally gotten a ticket to this event just to antagonize Nico? If so, that hurt — I thought we were friends. Also, why was Nico such a jerk to everyone? What was in that cocktail glass? Liquid didn't glow like that. Did Nico possess some kind of magic? Or was that some kind of trendy liqueur?

And why the heck wasn't he wearing a shirt? It was hot out but the air conditioning was working perfectly here in the inn. I watched as he pulsed his pectoral muscles while holding the cocktail glass.

Clara sidled up to me. "The look on your face is priceless. It's exactly how I feel," she whispered.

I instantly relaxed my facial muscles, realizing they were twisted into a skeptical grimace. Oh dear. Sometimes it was difficult for me to hide my emotions. I leaned into her. "This is much weirder than even I anticipated. Sorry."

"No worries. It's more entertaining than staying in a chain hotel off the interstate."

For some reason, this made me giggle. Then Clara giggled. Nico shot us a murderous glare.

"Ladies," he said icily, "if you're finished?" He raised his voice. "As I was saying, before being so rudely interrupted by the peanut gallery..."

"Sorry," Clara and I murmured in tandem, which only made us want to laugh more. Something about the tension, the absurdity of his leather pants, and the theatrical seriousness of it all had given us a case of inappropriate giggles.

I tried to focus on a row of books, but Jenny was standing nearby. The way she was pressing her lips together, trying not to laugh, made me want to double over. I bit the inside of my cheek and tried to focus on Nico without dissolving into hysterics.

"Tonight," Nico continued, holding his glowing blue cocktail aloft, "I bring you not merely dinner, but art. Innovation. Drama." He gestured at us, his audience. "Starting with this amuse-bouche of genuine fugu, prepared by yours truly. Farm-raised, as requested."

He gave me a hard stare and I smirked back. Jerk.

Kristan stood. She started to say something about how honored the Chamber was to host him as the first of seven pop-up dinners, but Nico steamrolled right over her. She melted back into the sofa, chastened. I felt terrible, because I knew how hard she'd worked on this entire event.

"But first, a toast." He raised his electric blue drink higher. "To all the small-town 'experts' who said I'd never make it. Who claimed I stole their techniques, their recipes, their wine knowledge." He stared pointedly on Adam. "This is what success looks like, people. Two million followers can't be—"

He broke off, his face flushing darker than the wine Mitzi had been guzzling. Something flickered in his eyes. I couldn't read his expression. Was it fear? Confusion? Revenge? The hand holding his cocktail trembled.

"I..." He pressed his free hand to his throat, the muscles in his bare chest tensing. "Need some... water. Kitchen. Nobody touch anything. I'll be right back to dazzle you all."

With that, he stormed through my hidden bookcase door toward the kitchen, his leather pants making angry little squeaking sounds. He continued to carry the plate of fish, but I noticed that he held it awkwardly, with none of the earlier flair.

Clara shifted beside me. "Is he always so dramatic?" she whispered.

"Dunno," I murmured back, taking a sip of my wine. Dang, that was tasty. I loved a good glass of pinot grigio.

"And people say women are histrionic," Clara said, raising her eyebrows and shaking her head.

We both snickered.

Around us, people started to chat. Mostly about the weather, which was beginning to sound ferocious outside. Someone mentioned they might need a canoe to get home.

Sarah Anderson, probably not used to the dramatic Florida weather, tugged her husband closer.

A loud crash echoed from the kitchen, followed by the distinctive sound of metal clanging on tile. I took another sip of wine and eyed Kristan, whose face was buried in her phone. Would the Chamber reimburse me for any damaged All-Clad pans?

"Should someone check on him?" Clara whispered.

I shrugged. At this point we could all hunker here, read from some of the witchy history books, and get drunk for all I cared. Maybe I should grab some cheese and crackers and call it a night.

Clara excused herself, saying she had to use the ladies' room.

Around us, the conversation continued, the noise level ticking up with each passing moment. What was happening with Nico? Maybe Clara was right, and I should ask if everything was okay. Honestly, I was kind of enjoying the vibe without Adam. It felt more like a cocktail party.

Mitzi was loudly telling the room about a ghost-hunting expedition in town that involved a Ouija board, a bottle of tequila, and a George Clooney lookalike. The newlyweds giggled. Adam yawned. I continued to drink.

Jenny came over to me.

"You okay?" I asked, reaching to squeeze her arm.

"Yeah, I mean, at least this isn't boring."

I wanted to hug her.

"Chef?" Ben's hesitant voice carried over the chatter. He stood in the doorway to my apartment, looking uncertain and a little afraid. Probably appropriate, given how Nico treated him. "Chef, do you need help with anything?"

When no response came, he disappeared into my apartment.

Jenny caught my eye. She gave a slight eye roll. I shrugged and gave her a *whaddyagonnado* expression. This dinner would either happen, or it wouldn't. I couldn't wait to hear people around town gossip about it.

Thunder rattled the windows. The storm was getting closer. I tried counting *one-one thousand, two-one thousand,* to determine how close it was to the house, but a strangled sound from the kitchen interrupted my concentration. Not a yell, more like a gasp. Ben appeared in the doorway to my apartment.

"Mrs., uh, Ms. Matthews? Amelia?" Ben's voice quavered. His face was drained of color, phone mount conspicuously absent. "Could you... could you come here for a moment?"

Ben grabbed my arm as I approached him, his fingers digging in with surprising strength. His breathing came in gulps.

"What's up?"

"In- in there," he managed, steering me through my apartment's hidden door.

As we passed through my living room, Ben's grip on my arm tightened. His face held something I couldn't quite read. Horror, yes, obviously. But also something else. For a split second, his shoulders dropped, like a weight had been lifted. Then the moment passed, and raw panic took over again.

"I'm sorry," he said, absolute panic in his wide eyes, "I think... I think..."

But I could already see past him into the kitchen. Nico lay on his side on my freshly mopped floor, one arm stretched out toward the sink. The blue cocktail glass had shattered beside him, its contents still glowing with an otherworldly light.

Freddie appeared in the doorway. He didn't just meow. He caterwauled. I looked from Freddie, to Nico, to Ben.

"Is he breathing?" I asked.

Ben shook his head. Freddie let out another wail.

Oh no. Not again.

Eleven

My body moved on autopilot, muscle memory from far too many similar situations kicking in. I dropped to my knees beside Nico, careful to avoid the puddle of eerily glowing blue liquid. Who knew what was in *that*.

By now, all of the guests had moved like a curious amoeba into my apartment. They peered in the kitchen, eager and curious.

"Everyone stand back!" I commanded, using what Jenny called my "mom voice." To my surprise, they listened. Even Adam stepped away from the scene, his earlier anger replaced by an expression of pure shock.

Murmurs and small gasps rippled through the crowd. Also, inexplicably, the pop of a bottle of wine. I looked up.

"Sorry," Mitzi said.

I shook my head and turned my attention back to Nico.

"I'm calling 911," Jenny said, her voice steady. My daughter pulled out her phone. Bless my calm girl. I heard her say "hello," and then she walked a few feet away as she explained the situation.

I pressed my fingers to Nico's neck, searching for a pulse while silently counting. Nothing. His skin was still warm, though his face remained frozen in that final expression of surprise. The muscles in his bare chest, which had been flexing for the camera only moments ago, were slack.

"Ben," I said, trying to keep my voice calm, "when was the last time he drank from that cocktail?"

The assistant gripped his phone mount. "He made it fresh right before coming out here. Said the glow effect only lasted twenty minutes. Something about the molecular structure of the—"

"Mom." Jenny's sharp voice interrupted Ben. "911 says emergency services might be delayed. The streets around downtown are flooded. They're sending someone as soon as they can but there's been some sort of electrical fire at a warehouse and all the units are there? I don't really get it."

Perfect. Just perfect.

The windows were shuddering in their frames from the thunder and wind. I glanced up, and realized all of the guests were congregating in my living room, sprawling on the sofa and chairs so they could get a peek at the tragedy unfolding in the kitchen.

Mitzi Blackwood took a long slug of wine. The Andersons huddled together, their ghost-hunting enthusiasm completely evaporated. Clara stood still, her face pale.

Only Kristan seemed composed, tapping rapidly on her phone. "I'm documenting everything for the Chamber's insurance." She looked up. "This is simply terrible, isn't it? Is he going to be okay?"

"It doesn't seem like it," I said.

I returned to Nico, my mind racing. The fish was scattered on the floor, the thin slices like pale petals. The plate was face down. The broken glass from his cocktail had scattered all over, fragments catching the kitchen's light like blue diamonds.

"Jenny," I said, rising slowly, "There's an emergency kit under the front desk. It's big and red. Can you bring it to me?"

She nodded and slipped out. I kept a well-stocked first aid kit, though it wouldn't help Nico now. What I needed was time to think.

"Everyone stay back, and please don't touch, well, anything," I announced to everyone, moving into the living room. "Not the fish, not the glass, not..." I gestured vaguely at Nico's body, still so absurd in those leather pants.

How was I going to handle this? I'd dealt with various, er, sticky situations in my nine months here, but never an actual body in my kitchen. I ripped my gaze away from Nico and scanned the group in my living room.

"Kristan," I called softly, catching her eye. "Could you help keep everyone comfortable in the dining room while I handle some things? Maybe see if there's any coffee left?"

She nodded briskly, already typing on her tablet. "Of course. I'll make sure no one wanders. Though I should note this is definitely not how I imagined our first pop-up dinner going." She gave a brittle laugh. "Do you need anything else?"

I searched her face, searching for any sign of tension beyond the obvious stress of the situation. "Keep everyone calm. And Kristan?"

"Hmm?"

She stepped into the kitchen and I leaned into her ear. "Have you noticed anything odd about Nico? Anything that worried you? Any health issues or something that would explain this?"

"Only that he was a complete jerk to everyone," she murmured, her professional composure cracking slightly. "I should have vetted him more thoroughly. The Chamber trusted me with this series and I..." She broke off, blowing out a tense breath.

"Got it," I said. Kristan stepped back into the living room.

"Shouldn't someone do CPR?" Sarah Anderson called out in a small voice.

I shook my head. After four murders in nine months, I knew death when I saw it. Though I couldn't exactly explain that to my guests without sounding like a complete ghoul. Also, I didn't want to have any contact with a potentially lethal substance, whether it be fugu or fire-blue cocktail.

"This is terrible." Clara poked her head in, then covered her mouth. "I was joking earlier about poisonous plants. I never thought this would happen right in front of me."

"No one did," Adam said grimly. He stood with his arms crossed, staring down at his nemesis. "Though some of us knew he was playing with fire."

I noticed Mitzi stepping around the body opening the fridge in the middle of all this, but didn't have the strength or time to ask her what she was doing. I noticed that she already had two boxes of crackers in her arms. What kind of guest did that under these circumstances? Unreal.

Kristan called Mitzi's name.

"Coming!" she trilled.

The nerve of some people. I shook my head.

Hoping against all odds, I pressed my fingers again to Nico's neck. Nothing. "Maybe he ate some of the fugu during prep?" I wondered aloud. "Could he have accidentally poisoned himself?"

"Impossible," Adam said firmly, stepping into the kitchen. "Fugu poisoning takes at least twenty minutes to kick in, usually longer. First you get numbness in your mouth, then paralysis starts in your limbs. The victim stays conscious until the end. This was too fast, too violent. And look at his face. He was in pain. Fugu victims kind of fade away."

I studied Nico's twisted expression. Adam was right. Whatever killed him had acted brutally fast. Fear crawled up my spine like an icy spider as a horrible realization dawned on me.

"Ben," I said, forcing my voice to stay steady, "was Nico on any medications? Any health conditions we should know about?"

Ben shifted uncomfortably. "I... I don't really know. He was pretty private about personal stuff."

Heart attacks could happen to young people, but given what Jenny said earlier about Nico's "biohacking," an inner voice told me that this wasn't a death from natural causes. Was this murder? I glanced at the faces around me.

Jenny returned with the first aid kit and something else:

Freddie had followed her, his orange tail held high. My cat took one look at Nico's body, hissed, and ran out. Just as well. I didn't want him around with the broken glass.

I watched Freddie's orange tail disappear around the corner into the library, then stood, brushing off my dress. My left knee twinged with pain, like it always did when it rained hard.

"Jenny," I said softly, touching my daughter's arm and leading her a few steps away. "I need you to do something important."

She nodded. Despite everything that had happened since she'd arrived — discovering her mom was a witch, meeting her mom's new boyfriend, and now witnessing a death — she was holding it together remarkably well. I couldn't be more proud of her.

My stomach churned with guilt. Less than twenty-four hours ago, my biggest worry had been explaining magic and Oliver to my daughter. Now I was potentially putting her in danger.

What if there was a killer in my inn, someone who'd murdered a man right in front of us? That person might be desperate enough to hurt anyone who got in their way. And here I was, asking my daughter to help.

Some mother I was turning out to be. Still. Jenny was my only ally under this roof, and I was determined to keep her safe. And there was safety in numbers. Wasn't that what all the Jessica Fletcher episodes taught me?

"Take everyone out of here, and into the dining room," I said, fighting to keep my voice steady. "Get some fresh bottles of wine. Not the ones Nico or Adam brought. Use the ones from our cabinet in the hallway. Keep them there until I, ah." I cleared my throat, not wanting to say "investigate the crime scene" to my daughter.

"Until you do your thing?" She blinked.

"My what?"

"Mom." She gave me a look that was pure teenager despite her being twenty-one. "I may think this whole witch situation is weird, but I'm not stupid. You said you have a psychic ability and that you solve crimes with your coven. Clearly you have some kind of..." she waved her hand vaguely "process, when these things happen."

I stared at her, touched by this weird mix of skepticism and faith, even as fear gnawed at my insides. I wanted to tell her to get in her car and drive far away from here. But with the streets flooding...

"Try to be careful," she added. "And, Mom, don't touch anything gross."

"Of course not." I squeezed her arm, perhaps a little too tightly. "Now go. Take them all to the dining room. Even Ben. Actually, especially Ben, since he seems to be in shock. And Jenny? Watch them. Note if anyone leaves to use the bathroom or makes a phone call. But," I swallowed hard. "Don't put yourself at risk. If anything feels wrong—"

"Mom." Her voice was gentle. "I've got this. And I've got my phone. One tap and I can text you. Or the cops. Although at this point I trust you more than the cops here, since they can't even respond to a guy dropping dead."

I blinked, unsure of how to respond. "Thanks, I guess," I finally said.

Once they filed out, I turned back to the body. Rain tapped against the windows, and thunder growled in the distance. My kitchen felt different now. It was heavy with the presence of death and secrets.

I pulled on a pair of latex gloves from the first aid kit. Then, carefully avoiding the spilled cocktail, I crouched next to Nico. His eyes bulged, staring sightlessly upward, reflecting the overhead light. His right hand was curled into a loose fist, and something glinted between his fingers.

Holding my breath, I gently pried them open. A pinky-finger sized crystal tumbled to the floor. It was green, almost the color of grass. I scooped it up.

The moment I did, the vision hit me like one of the violent lightning bolts flashing in the sky.

Twelve

The moment my fingers touched the green crystal, the vision took hold. I was in the back room of the Astral Attic, where my friend Liz kept the more dangerous items. Clara moved between shelves of deadly herbs, her movements quick and furtive.

A wicker basket with wire handles was suspended in the crook of her arm. Yep, those were the small shopping baskets at the Attic. Inside Clara's basket was the green crystal, along with a few other stones.

Clara wore the same outfit as when she'd arrived at the inn, suggesting this took place in the afternoon. The air smelled like grass, moss, and mingled herbs. Clara stopped to inspect a jar.

Something felt wrong. These weren't cooking herbs or medicinal plants. The jars bore skull-and-crossbones labels: LETHAL IF INGESTED. HANDLE WITH EXTREME CARE.

I recognized the contents. *Foxglove. Nightshade. Oleander.* Fast-acting poisons that could be easily masked in food or drink.

Clara consulted a leather-bound journal, its pages marked with dozens of colored tabs. Her normally gentle face was hard with concentration as she made notes with precise, sharp strokes.

"Perfect," she murmured, selecting a small vial. "Fast-acting. Untraceable. Precisely what I need for my big demonstration."

What was she going to demonstrate?

Lightning flashed in both the vision and reality as I watched her pay, tucking the vials and journal into her purse. The vision released me with a jolt, leaving me breathless and shaken.

My head throbbed, a common aftereffect of my intense visions. But this time, the pain felt secondary to the horror of what I'd witnessed. Had I witnessed Clara planning Nico's murder?

Thought after thought flew through my brain as I tried to make sense of what I'd seen in the vision. Earlier, Clara had seemed so genuine, so wounded by her divorce. She'd been earnestly excited about her flower truck venture, about starting over on Florida's Gulf Coast. Nothing about her demeanor suggested she was capable of murder.

But then again, I'd learned during my time in Cypress Grove that people were complicated. Sometimes the most seemingly gentle souls harbored the darkest secrets.

Still, why would Clara want to kill Nico? It made no sense. They weren't the same age. She didn't look like a TikTok influencer. She'd barely met him. Unless. Had something happened during cocktail hour that I'd missed? Had he said something cruel to her, triggered something from her past?

Or did the two of them somehow know each other? My mind raced with possibilities and connections. Clara knew Kristan, who had invited Nico. Hmm.

"Mom?"

I gasped, startled, nearly jumping out of my skin at Jenny's voice. Scrambling on the floor like a crab, I twisted my body and turned to face her. She was standing in the doorway, eyes wide and face devoid of color.

"Mom, what's wrong? Are you okay? Oh my God. Did you touch that blue stuff? Did you—"

I lumbered to my feet. "Honey, no. I'm okay. Well, my knee is a little wonky. You know how it gets."

She shook her head vigorously. "No, you're not okay. You

looked like you were in a trance. Or hypnotized. Were you talking to yourself? It looked like you were in some other realm or something. Mom, it was scary."

Then, she burst into tears.

"Oh, honey." I slipped the green crystal into my dress pocket and went to my daughter. Instinctively, I put my arm around her, leading her out of the kitchen and into the privacy — and safety — of my living room. I quickly shut the bookcase door that led to the inn. Maybe I should keep her in here while I handled the guests and the body and the authorities.

Whenever they decided to show up. Then again, no. I didn't want to leave her here with Nico's body in the next room. The idea of that was far too grim. Perhaps I should send her to a guest room upstairs.

For the moment, I made her sit with me on the sofa. Freddie emerged from the hall and jumped into Jenny's lap. He began purring, and she worked her hands into his long, orange fur.

"Jenny, I know this is a traumatic experience. It's going to be okay." I wasn't sure if I entirely believed that; after all, there might be a killer sitting and drinking wine in my dining room right this very moment. From what I'd seen in my vision, all signs pointed to Clara. "This is so much for someone so young. I'm sorry, sweetheart."

Sweet, confused Clara. I wanted to poke around and talk to the guests, wanted to find out if my hunch was true. But I had to first soothe my daughter. She was now sobbing.

"It is a lot, but that's not why I'm..." she gasped for breath. "It's everything. I'm so freaked out."

"Understandable. A young man collapsed and died. It's not something you get used—"

"No, it's not that. It's Sedona." She sniffled and I looked around helplessly for a tissue. There were none in here, and I didn't want to leave her alone to run into the bathroom. Not when she was this upset.

I took my long, flowy sleeve and dabbed at her tears. "Huh? Sedona?"

"Sedona," she repeated. "That's why I'm here early. That's why I showed up at the festival. I couldn't, I couldn't stay in Arizona anymore."

Thunder cracked overhead, making us both jump. Freddie remained unperturbed, kneading Jenny's leg as if trying to comfort her.

"What happened in Sedona, pumpkin?" I asked softly, another layer of fear lodging into my chest. I knew something was definitely off because Jenny didn't even correct me when I used my childhood pet name for her.

Jenny took a shuddering breath. "A couple of weekends ago, my friend Brittany and I went to Sedona to hike. Remember, I told you we were going there?"

I nodded. "Yes, you sent me photos of a cactus."

"Right. Well, we went to Cathedral Rock. We stayed until after dark because the stars are supposed to be amazing there." She paused, her hands tightening in Freddie's fur. "And they were. Until they moved."

I waited, my heart pounding. Outside, the storm raged, but in here, time seemed to slow. I blinked. Didn't all stars move? I wasn't up on my astronomy. "Okay?"

"At first I thought it was satellites. You know how you can track the ISS on your phone?" Her voice quavered.

I nodded, but actually, I didn't know anything about satellites, never mind the ISS.

"But then the lights started moving in patterns. Making shapes. And I could... I could understand them, Mom. Like they were talking to me. I couldn't handle it."

I froze.

My throat felt tight. No wonder she'd shown up out of nowhere. No wonder she'd been so thrown by my own supernatural revelations. She'd been wrestling with something far stranger than psychometry or crystal grids.

"Oh, sweetheart." The words came out as barely a whisper. I gathered her in my arms like I had when she was little, squashing Freddie a little in the process. Thankfully, he kept purring. I rocked her gently, then she pulled away. Then it hit me, how she acted while we were downtown. "Is that why you kept looking at the sky earlier today?"

She nodded. "I know how it sounds. I can't help but check, everywhere I go."

"What happens to you? What's it like?"

"You actually believe me?" She let out an incredulous snort. "Well, of course you do."

"Of course I do," I repeated insistently. "Now tell me what you see and feel. I need to know so I can try to help."

"I thought I was having some kind of altitude sickness. Or maybe someone had slipped something into my water bottle." She gave a brittle laugh. "But it kept happening. Every night. Even back in my dorm. Lights, Messages. Sometimes right in my head, sometimes in the sky. Early one morning I was up, and I looked out my dorm window, and the lights were there. Then two days ago, I woke up and my entire room was filled with this weird blue light, and I couldn't deal. I had to get out of there."

"That sounds terrifying." My breath came in short, sharp gasps. The idea that anyone — human, ghost, extraterrestrial — would frighten my daughter made me want to rage at the world. "What kind of messages?"

"They weren't like words," she continued, her voice dropping to almost a whisper. "More like downloads? Like when your phone updates but it's your brain. Coordinates. Star maps. Things I couldn't possibly understand but somehow did."

She tapped her right temple. "And the worst part? I started seeing patterns everywhere. In my textbooks, in traffic lights, even on TikTok. Like everything was trying to tell me something."

"Did the messages feel threatening?" I asked softly, taking her hand into both of mine.

"No. That's what's so weird. They felt... felt..." She searched for the word. "Important. Urgent. Like when you know you've forgotten something crucial but can't remember what." She looked at me with red-rimmed eyes. "I couldn't sleep. Couldn't focus. How am I supposed to focus on summer classes when I'm getting cosmic downloads about. About..."

"About what?"

"I don't even know. That's what scared me the most. Like I was being prepared for something, but I don't know what."

My mind spun with questions. What kind of messages? Where were they coming from? Had she told anyone else? But most of all, my heart ached with guilt. While I'd been here discovering my own powers, surrounded by a supportive coven and friends who understood, my daughter had been alone with something that petrified her. Why hadn't she called me?

She looked up at me, tears streaming down her face. "And now I find out you're part of some witch coven? And you see visions? I've been fighting so hard not to believe in any of this stuff, trying to convince myself I was stressed about finals or something. But seeing you just now, in that trance..." She shuddered. "I don't know what to think anymore. I'm sorry if I was a jerk about your abilities or powers or whatever when I first got here. It scared me, honestly. Considering what I've been going through. I didn't mean it. It's kinda cool that you're a witch even though it's weird. But everything is so... unsettling."

"Oh, baby." I swallowed a big lump in my throat, fighting back tears and so many fears. *This is really happening to my child.*

Jenny shuddered in a breath. "Maybe I'm more like you than I thought."

I'd had similarly horrifying thoughts about my own mother, but they hadn't involved extraterrestrials. Holy crap. I had to stay strong for Jenny.

"Have you, um." I swallowed, choosing my words carefully. "Have you seen anything unusual in the sky since you arrived here?"

"No. Thank goodness. Nothing. It's like it all stopped when I got to Florida. I got a great night's sleep last night. So maybe I really am losing my mind."

"You're not losing anything," I said firmly, though my own brain was racing. My daughter was communicating with UFOs. My practical, skeptical daughter who'd spent the last twenty-four hours rolling her eyes at my crystals and herb bundles was receiving messages from somewhere in the sky.

And we had a dead man in the kitchen and maybe a killer in the dining room. Just peachy.

"Mom, there's something else."

I swallowed hard. How much more could I handle? "Okay?"

"Before I left, I withdrew from school. Not only my summer class, but the entire program. That's why I didn't tell you this before. I was afraid you'd be mad. I acted really impulsively, but I can't go back there. I'm not going back." She pressed her face into Freddie's neck and wiped her nose on his fur. He didn't seem to mind, and that was the least of my worries right now.

"Withdrew from school?" My head spun. Jenny had only two semesters left, not counting the summer school class. "Honey, I'm not mad. I'm worried about you. And right now I'm worried about keeping you safe tonight, right now. We can deal with everything else later. I want you to stay in here with Freddie. I'm sure the police or the ambulance or somebody will be here soon."

They had to, right? They didn't ignore reports of a man dropping dead.

She shook her head. "No way. I'm not letting you go back in there alone." Jenny scratched behind Freddie's ears. "What if someone killed Nico? And what if they decide to, I don't know, poison the wine next?"

I winced. "I've handled murderers before," I said, then immediately regretted it when her eyes widened. "I mean—"

"Before? Mom, exactly how many murders have you solved? How involved have you really been in these investigations? I can't believe I'm asking this."

I caught myself counting on my fingers and quickly dropped

my hands to my lap. "That's not important right now. What's important is that you stay here where it's safe while I—"

"While you what? Have a cocktail party and investigate with a bunch of suspects?" She crossed her arms. "Yeah, no. Not happening."

"Jenny—"

"Mom."

We stared at each other. I recognized that stubborn set of her jaw. It was mine, after all.

"Look," I tried again, "dealing with murderers is one thing. But you've got enough on your plate with..." I waved my hand vaguely at the ceiling, immediately feeling foolish. What was I pointing at? The sky? Space?

"With my alien problem?" Her mouth twitched. "At least I'm not the one who talks to ghost cats."

"That was an isolated incident!" I protested. "And she was a very nice ghost cat who belonged to a kind old spirit. Who made excellent biscuits, by the way."

"What was the ghost cat's name?" Jenny challenged me, as if she still didn't believe me.

"Coco."

Freddie's head popped up at the mention of his buddy from another realm. I wanted to tell Jenny about how he could see Coco the ghost cat, and often chased her around the apartment. (At least, I thought it was her. Who knew how many ghost pets were running around this place?)

"See?" Jenny scratched under his chin. "Even Freddie thinks we should stick together. Besides, I've seen every true crime show on Netflix. I could help."

"Absolutely not. This isn't some TV show, this is real. And we don't know for sure if Nico was murdered."

A burble of voices wafted into the room. I detected Adam's baritone. "The National Weather Service has posted a tornado warning for the east part of the county..."

Jenny and I looked at each other.

"Fine," I sighed. "But you stay next to me at all times. And if I tell you to run—"

"I know, I know. Run and don't look back." She stood, displacing an annoyed Freddie. "I've seen horror movies too, Mom."

"This isn't funny."

"Then why are you smiling?"

Because somehow, despite everything — the murder, the storm, the UFOs — having my daughter by my side made me feel stronger.

"Come on," I said instead. "Let's go see what fresh chaos awaits us. And Jenny?"

"Yeah?"

"We're going to talk about this whole dropping out of college thing later. Did you tell your father yet?" I suspected she hadn't, since I hadn't gotten an irate email from him.

Chad was going to lose his mind when he heard about this. And since he was paying for it, I had to brace for a battle of epic proportions. How would I explain this to him? But there was no way in the universe I was sending Jenny back to Arizona.

This was a problem for future me. I rubbed my eyes.

She groaned. "No, I didn't tell Dad. Can we focus on solving one life-altering crisis at a time?"

Thirteen

After agreeing that yes, we would solve the most immediate problem first — the dead chef in the other room — we decided to get organized.

The two of us locked Freddie in the bedroom with some water and kibble, then returned to the kitchen. We came to a halt, with Jenny peeking around me, both staring at Nico's body. The blue liquid from his last cocktail still glowed eerily. Because of the storm outside, the lights flickered.

"We should cover him," Jenny whispered. "It feels wrong, leaving him like that."

I nodded. In my rush to get everyone out, I'd left him exposed. I went into the living room, my eyes landing on a black, yellow, and green crocheted afghan draped over a wingback chair. "That might work," I said, pointing. "If it's big enough."

Jenny retrieved it and hesitated. "Should we really be doing this? I mean, for evidence and stuff?"

I screwed up my face. "Well, um."

I thought about the other crime scenes I'd encountered since inheriting the inn. "We're not disturbing anything. We're help-ing." I gestured at Nico's bare chest, which looked almost waxy in the wan light. "Giving him some peace."

A burst of laughter floated in from the dining room, followed by what sounded like Mitzi attempting to sing "Don't Stop Believin'."

My eyes met my daughter's and we both winced.

"Pretty sure she's hammered," I said.

"Nightmare fuel," she added. I wasn't entirely sure what that meant, but I agreed with the sentiment.

Together, we shook out the afghan. My aunt had bought it at an estate sale years ago — I'd seen that memory when I first touched it. The old woman who'd crocheted it had made it as a wedding gift for her granddaughter. She never could have imagined it would be used like this. Honestly, I thought it was kind of ugly but I'd kept it around for some reason.

Now I knew why.

The thing barely covered Nico. At first we pulled it up to his chin, like he was sleeping. Probably we should find a sheet, but that small task seemed insurmountable at the moment. The afghan would have to do.

"That's not right," I said, pulling the sheet to cover his face. "There. I think that's better."

"But then his feet stick out." She glanced at his feet, which were clad in expensive-looking black leather boots. "Ugh. His eyes are still open."

I sighed, fighting back memories of the other bodies I'd encountered during my time in Cypress Grove. This part never got easier. "Well, then his feet will stick out. Nothing we can do about that."

Thunder shook the old building hard enough to make the glasses left on the tables tinkle. In the dining room, someone squealed.

Jenny touched my arm as we stared down at the now-covered body. "What do we do now?"

Another burst of laughter floated in from the dining room, followed by what sounded suspiciously like Mitzi Blackwood launching into "Sweet Caroline."

I sighed. "Now we go deal with that, in there."

"Freaks," Jenny whispered.

Before we headed to the dining room, I pulled Jenny aside into a quiet corner of the library, far from both Nico and the increasingly raucous sounds from down the hall.

"There's something I need to tell you," I whispered, glancing around to make sure we were alone. "When I touched that crystal that fell from Nico's hand, I had a vision. When you saw me zoned out before, that's what was going on."

Jenny's eyebrows shot up. "Like, a real vision? Not just vibes?" She waggled her fingers.

Before I could respond, Mitzi's voice carried into the room. "Has anyone seen my fountain pen? It's a Montblanc, gold?"

I peered into the dining room. She was digging through her designer clutch, setting lipsticks, loose change, and some wadded up tissues on the table. "I set it down somewhere. I wanted to show everyone how it detects spiritual energy. It's been in my family for generations."

Turning back to Jenny, I hissed. "A real vision. Not necessarily bad vibes, but ominous ones. I saw Clara in a store in downtown Cypress Grove. She was holding an arsenic vial, making notes about toxic dried herbs in some kind of journal, talking about how flowers could be weapons. I know Nico could've died from natural causes but I can't help but feel he was killed, possibly by Clara."

"Clara?" Jenny's jaw dropped. "But she seems so sweet! And weren't we helping her feel welcome, like, a couple of hours ago?"

I nodded grimly. "I know. That's what makes this difficult. But the vision was clear. And her whole fascination with true crime is odd, don't you think?"

"Mom, no." Jenny shook her head vigorously. "She was talking about true crime podcasts. That's totally different from actually murdering someone. Most women like true crime podcasts. It's all about facing our fears, how we're at a physical disadvantage to men, and how we're subverting that by learning more about what harms us."

While I was proud of my daughter and her meta-feminist learnings, this wasn't the time to unpack all that. A whiff of lavender drifted between us, and I wondered which of my guests was wearing the perfume. It was oddly comforting in the midst of all this chaos.

Another peal of laughter echoed from the dining room, followed by a crash and Mitzi's distinctive "Oopsie!"

"Right. Well. People kill for all sorts of reasons, and we don't really know what anyone's capable of. We don't know anyone's background here." I paused, thinking of Adam and his animosity toward Nico. "Let's get in there. But first, I need you to help me watch Clara carefully. Note if she says anything suspicious or tries to leave. Be subtle about it."

A flash of lightning illuminated the library. We both looked at the open door into the apartment, probably both thinking about what lay inside.

"Fine," Jenny sighed. "I'll help you spy on Clara. But for the record, I still think you're wrong about her."

"Noted. Also, I want to make a quick call."

"Oh, to 911 again?"

I inhaled sharply. "Well, no, but that's a good idea. Why don't you do that while I try to phone someone in town who might be able to come over to help?"

"Your man?"

I blinked. "Hunh?"

"Your boyfriend. The cute nerdy guy."

"Oh. Yes. I'm going to call Oliver. The cute nerdy guy."

I reached into my pocket for my phone and tapped Oliver's contact info. I hesitated for a second. There was no way I wanted him to drive in this weather. I knew if I called him, he'd abandon his jam session in a heartbeat to come here.

But I needed help, and common sense won out. Oliver had a

rational, calming presence and if any group needed that, it was the one in my dining room. I dialed.

I frowned at my cell screen as the call failed to connect. "That's weird." I tried again, but got nothing. Not even a ring. Silence. The third time, my phone displayed "Call Failed" before returning to the home screen. I groaned.

Jenny watched me, her own phone in hand. "No luck?"

"The cell network must be down." I chewed on my cheek while staring at the one bar in the corner of my screen. It flickered away for a few seconds. There was signal, but it was weak and the calls weren't going through. "Maybe the towers got overloaded with the storm."

"Let me try 911 again." Jenny tapped her screen, then shook her head. "Nothing. Not even an emergency connection." She looked up at me, and I saw a flicker of fear cross her face. "Mom?"

Thunder crashed overhead, and the library lights dimmed for a long moment before brightening again.

I reached for Jenny's arm, and she grabbed mine. Neither of us said it, but we were both thinking the same thing: we were trapped in a house with a possible killer, no way to call for help, and a storm that was getting worse by the minute.

"Well," I whispered, trying to sound more confident than I felt, "let's try to keep everyone calm in the meantime."

Together, we left the room. Jenny's grip on my arm tightened as we walked down the dark hallway toward the dining room.

The dining table had transformed from the elegant spread Jenny had created into something from a Bacchanal.

The carefully arranged place settings were askew, wine glasses scattered across the damask tablecloth in various states of emptiness. Crimson stains dotted the linens. Someone had knocked over the pineapple centerpiece, and its cheerful green and yellow glazing now seemed garishly out of place.

Mitzi Blackwood held court at one end of the table, her designer dress slipping off her wide-shouldered frame, waving a nearly-empty wine glass as she regaled the Andersons with what appeared to be a ghost story. Her face was flushed, and she'd kicked off one of her expensive shoes.

She was also looking at Marc Anderson like he was a tasty snack.

The young couple sat close together, looking shell-shocked but politely attentive. Sarah kept glancing at the doorway as if expecting Nico to walk in and announce it had all been a prank. Marc's hand was in Sarah's, and he kept glancing with more than a little fear in his eyes at Mrs. Blackwood.

Adam stood by the window, staring out at the storm, his own wine glass untouched. Which I thought was a little odd for a man who owned a wine bar. His jaw was set in a hard line, and he kept checking his phone and shaking his head.

A makeshift charcuterie board had materialized: chunks of my good aged cheddar, an imported Italian salami I'd bought for my weekly movie night with Oliver, and what looked like every cracker in my pantry arranged on a silver serving plate. That must have been Mitzi when she raided my fridge.

Clara sat alone in the corner, arms wrapped around her midsection, barely touching her glass of red wine. She looked small and lost, exactly like someone who'd recently witnessed a murder.

Or exactly like someone who'd committed one, depending on how you looked at it.

Ben huddled near the door, still clutching his phone rig, though he'd stopped filming. His face was pale, and he kept looking toward the library. He waved me over, and Jenny followed.

"Is everything okay?" he asked.

I opened my mouth, then closed it. An odd question, but I figured the kid was probably in shock. "Uh, well. Things are pretty much the same, I guess."

Only Kristan seemed semi-composed, tapping away at her tablet with a deep frown. She'd positioned herself near a power outlet and had somehow procured both a phone charger and a portable battery pack.

"Everything downtown is flooded," she announced, then stared at me. "I've been keeping everyone up-to-date on the weather. Are the paramedics on their way?"

She took a sip of a large glass of white wine.

"Sure are," I lied, wanting everyone to think I had this under control. Frankly, everyone in this room seemed highly suspect all of a sudden. I raised my voice. "The cops, too."

Jenny squeezed my arm as another bolt of lightning sliced through the night. "Mom," she whispered.

Before I could respond, Mitzi's voice rang out: "Amelia! Jenny! Come join us! I was telling everyone about the time I was at a séance and we conjured the ghost of Ponce de Leon. Though I suppose that's nothing compared to tonight's excitement!"

I winced at her choice of words. Next to me, Jenny muttered, "Yikes."

Running my tongue over my teeth, I surveyed the room, trying to make sense of it all. Mitzi's loud ghost stories, Adam's brooding silence, the Andersons' stunned politeness.

Everyone was processing what had happened in their own way. I reminded myself that shock and grief took different forms. Some people got quiet, others got drunk, and apparently some raided their hostess's cheese drawer.

Still, everything felt way off about the whole scene. Like we were all actors in some strange play, each performing our assigned roles. The grieving assistant, the drunk socialite, the shellshocked honeymoon couple. Even Clara's solitary vigil in the corner seemed almost too perfect.

For the first time since moving to Cypress Grove, I felt truly alone. Usually when weird things happened — and to be sure, weird things happened a lot in this town — I had backup. I had people who knew more than I did about the supernatural and about death.

Oliver should be here with his encyclopedic knowledge of Florida folklore and crime. Liz would have already cleansed the space with herbs and set up protective crystals. Sage would be grilling everyone with nonstop questions. Even Jimbo, who was probably line-dancing with Sage somewhere in Montana, would have been a calming presence with his uniquely Florida wisdom such as, "If psychedelic mushrooms can grow in poop, so can you."

But they weren't here. It was only me and Jenny, trying to figure out how a man died while keeping a house full of traumatized guests safe during a storm. I glanced at my daughter, who was eyeing the deteriorating situation with a poised, calm expression. Maybe I wasn't as alone as I thought.

Another flash of lightning illuminated the room, followed almost immediately by a thunderclap that made everyone jump. The lights flickered once again.

"Mom," Jenny whispered again, "maybe we should—"

But Mitzi's voice drowned her out: "Amelia! You simply must tell everyone about the ghost in your attic! The one that gave the former mayor a heart attack!"

I closed my eyes briefly. This was going to be a very long night. Where were the paramedics? The police? Nico was beyond help, but were we?

Fourteen

"Maybe we should start by talking to Adam," I whispered to Jenny while trying to tamp down my mounting fear. "He seems the most sober."

"Unlike some people," Jenny muttered, eyeing Mitzi, who was now attempting to teach Marc Anderson something she claimed was an "ancient Floridian rain dance."

"Honey, that's the Macarena. Let's not," Sarah Anderson said weakly, tugging at her husband's sleeve.

As we slowly shuffled toward Adam, I paused to grab a couple of crackers and some cheese. My stomach was growling, and I'd spent fifteen bucks on this aged cheddar.

Jenny reached for my arm as I munched. "Mom," she whispered, "is it just me, or is Mitzi weirdly... happy? Like, there's a dead guy in the kitchen and she's acting like she's at a bachelorette party."

I glanced at Mitzi. She'd kicked off her other shoe and was trying to convince Ben to film her while dancing "for the inevitable Netflix series." Her face was flushed, and she kept smoothing her designer dress while clearing her throat.

"Yeah," I murmured. "Though some people get inappropriate

when they're in shock. Remember your Aunt Susan at Nana Mary's funeral?"

Jenny snorted. "You mean when she started telling everyone about her C-section?"

"Exactly." Though Mitzi's behavior did seem odd, even for someone in shock. I filed that away for later consideration.

We reached Adam, who was still staring out the window at the storm. Lightning illuminated his face, highlighting the tension in his jaw. I cleared my throat.

"So, Adam—"

"SWEET CAROLINE!" Mitzi's voice cut through the room. "BAH BAH BAHHH!"

Adam winced. I tried again. "Adam, I was wondering if you'd noticed anything about—"

"GOOD TIMES..." the rest came out garbled.

"So good?" Ben joined in weakly, perhaps hoping to prevent Mitzi from climbing onto the table and doing a go-go dance, which she looked about ready to do. Or he was just that traumatized, he'd go along with anything. Who knew? Kristan shot Mitzi a dirty look.

Jenny tugged at my sleeve. "Mom, maybe we should—"

"Mitzi!" I called out, my voice sharper than intended. "Perhaps we could keep it down a bit? Out of respect? For the deceased? I know everyone's a little emotional right now, but let's hold it together."

She paused mid-sway, wine sloshing dangerously close to my vintage tablecloth. "Oh! Of course, darling. So sorry." She stage-whispered to the Andersons: "We should be more respectful of the recently departed. Because he did have amazing abs."

Sarah Anderson choked on her wine.

I turned back to Adam, determined to get some information. "As I was saying, I couldn't help but notice Clara seems a bit overwhelmed."

Adam huffed out a cynical laugh. "We're all overwhelmed, Amelia. A man keeled over and died in your kitchen."

"True, but—"

"Though some of us are handling it better than others." He shot a pointed look at Mitzi, who was flashing her upper thigh at Marc while saying something about the "real Moulin Rouge, the one in Paris."

More dramatic thunder, more flashes of light. In the corner, Clara huddled deeper into herself, looking small and vulnerable. Maybe too vulnerable? I surreptitiously eyeballed her. Why wasn't she next to Kristan, her friend?

"Did you happen to talk with Clara earlier?" I tried to sound casual. "Before everything happened?"

"Not really. We introduced ourselves and she told me about her flower truck. I mentioned Grape Escape and we were discussing wine. You know, the usual small talk." He paused. "Actually, she asked a lot of questions about different types of—"

"WHO LET THE DOGS OUT?" Mitzi had apparently moved on to a new song. "WHO? NEWSFLASH! I LET THE DOGS OUT! Or was it *you*, Jennifer?"

Mitzi shut one eye and fixed the other on my daughter.

"Not me, bestie!" Jenny called out in a cheery voice, then leaned close to my ear and spoke between gritted teeth. "Mom, she's getting worse."

"Bestie," Mitzi burbled. "That's so adorable. We're besties!"

I watched Mitzi more carefully. Her movements were becoming more erratic, her eyes slightly unfocused and kind of glossy. Something definitely wasn't right. But before I could process that thought, a massive thunderclap shook the inn, and the lights went out.

We weren't plunged into darkness. We belly flopped into it.

Several people screamed. I heard Mitzi's throaty voice: "Ooh, now it's a proper séance!"

"Everyone stay calm," I called out, though my own heart was racing and I was anything but relaxed. I felt my way along the wall toward the banquette where I kept emergency supplies. My hip bumped into something, but I kept going until my hands found the familiar drawer handle. Inside should be votive candles, and I knew Aunt Shirley's old Zippo lighter would be there too.

But when my fingers searched the drawer, the lighter wasn't there. The candles were, but no flame. Weird.

"Does anyone have a light?" I asked.

"Oh! Oh! I do!" Mitzi's voice came through the darkness, followed by the sound of her rummaging through her purse. "Here we go. I use it for my, um, medicinal herbs. For my glaucoma, you know." She tittered. "Sometimes a lady needs her wacky tabacky."

I heard someone's sharp intake of breath and a muttered "what a piece of work." I think it was Adam who said that.

"Wait, I've got my cell flashlight," Kristan announced, a beam cutting through the darkness. Several more people followed her lead and I was awash in light, like I was on stage at a small rock concert.

"Let me light these, so we don't use up our phone batteries," I said.

Mitzi pressed something cool and plastic into my hand. The moment my fingers closed around the cheap Bic lighter, a vision hit me: Mitzi in her garden, wearing silk pajamas, giggling while smoking something that definitely wasn't tobacco. The vision faded as quickly as it came.

I flicked the lighter, and the flame cast strange shadows on the walls. One by one, I lit the votives, setting them in glass holders carefully around the room. Everyone extinguished their phone lights.

"You know what would make this party really fun?" Mitzi reached into her purse again and extracted a baggie. "I've got a little something we could all share. Takes the edge right off."

"Mitzi!" Sarah Anderson's scandalized gasp cut through the room.

"What?" Mitzi blinked innocently. "It's legal now in Florida. Mostly. Sort of. Besides, we could all use some relaxation, what with the dead chef and everything."

I heard Clara's quiet "oh my word" from the corner, while Adam muttered something that sounded like "this cannot be happening."

"Mom?" Jenny sidled up to me. "Remember what you said about people acting weird when they're in shock?"

"Yeah?"

"I don't think this is shock."

In the serene candlelight, Mitzi was now attempting to climb onto the antique sideboard, declaring she needed a "better stage" for her performance.

"Nope," Jenny muttered. "Definitely not shock."

I squeezed her hand, my mind racing. I wanted to talk with everyone privately, but Mitzi's increasingly concerning behavior was making that impossible. Plus, something about her reaction felt wrong.

Very wrong.

The storm raged outside, and in the distance, I heard what sounded like tornado sirens. Or maybe it was an ambulance? I sent a silent prayer to the universe and all of the goddesses above.

"Help me get her down," I whispered to Jenny. "Then maybe we can try talking to the Andersons. They were near Clara during part of the cocktail hour."

Mitzi belted out another tune, somehow having acquired another full glass of wine.

Jenny pressed her hands into her hips. "Maybe we should make some coffee first."

"Lots of coffee," I agreed. And perhaps I should corral Mitzi into a guest room, although I didn't want her trashing it. "Take her in the library and don't let her anywhere near Nico, okay?"

Jenny nodded.

As she moved to rescue my furniture from Mitzi's inappropriate exuberance, I noticed Clara watching us with an unreadable expression. Was it guilt? Fear? Or something else entirely?

Jenny, using a well of patience I didn't know she possessed, steered Mitzi toward the library with promises of a comfy place to stretch out.

I let out a breath. As much as I didn't want Jenny out of my sight, I also figured my daughter could take the intoxicated Mitzi down if needed. This gave me a chance to focus.

I went over to Clara and squeezed her arm. "Hey, lady. How are you holding up? I'm so sorry you had to see this."

"Don't apologize, it's not your fault."

We exchanged sad looks, but inside, I was questioning every detail.

"Amelia, this is embarrassing," she whispered, "but I bought several protective crystals today, before I came here. It was at a place called The Astral Attic, a store Kristan recommended. A cute shop downtown."

My breath hitched. "Yes, I know the store."

She twisted her hands. "They're gone. The crystals. I had them in my purse, but now, I can't find them." She swallowed hard. "I know it seems silly to worry about missing crystals when someone died, but I've got a strange feeling."

A chill flowed through me. First my salt, then Mitzi's fountain pen, and now Clara's crystal. Wait, and what about the Zippo lighter? Four missing mystical objects in one evening couldn't be a coincidence. And one of them had been in the hand of a dead man.

"You're not the only one with a strange feeling." I sighed and sank next to her into a chair, keeping my voice low while I made a quick decision. Something about Clara's demeanor, her genuine concern about the crystals, her big, blue eyes that were both wary and skittish.

It made me want to trust her. But I couldn't. Not yet.

I leaned closer, pretending to examine a water stain on the tablecloth. "Listen," I whispered, "I need to tell you something, and it's going to sound very odd. Crazy, even."

Clara gave me a lopsided, tired smile, then glanced around and lowered her voice to match mine. "Stranger than a shirtless chef dropping dead at a dinner party during a tropical storm?"

"Maybe." I did another quick scan of the room. Adam was still brooding by the window, and the Andersons had huddled together in the far corner, whispering to each other. Kristan appeared absorbed in her tablet, but her fingers hadn't moved on the screen for several minutes. I shifted my chair closer to Clara's, using the next rumble of thunder as cover. Ben was slumped against the chair, his eyes closed.

"You mentioned the Astral Attic," I murmured. "You bought dried herbs while you were there, didn't you? Including arsenic."

A little gasp escaped her mouth. "How did you...?" She broke off as Kristan looked up at us. We both pretended to study the rain hitting the windows until Kristan returned to her tablet.

"I know about the herbs because I saw you buying them. I have an ability. Psychometry. I can see visions when I touch certain objects."

"Oh?" she breathed. "That's wild." Her eyes flitted around the room. We sat in silence for a few minutes, the candlelight casting a warm glow around the room.

Then she touched my wrist with long, slim fingers. "Wait. Can you.... Would you be willing to try something?"

She reached into her purse and pulled out a small, worn leather notebook, the kind that has changeable paper inserts. "This was my grandmother's. She gave it to me right before she died. I've carried it every day since. Would you be able to discern anything from it?"

Appreciating her desire to fact-check my abilities, I took the notebook carefully. It was the one I'd seen her consult in my earlier vision.

The moment my fingers touched the soft, brown leather, a vision engulfed me: An elderly woman with Clara's blue eyes, sitting in a hospital bed. She pressed the notebook into young Clara's hands, whispering "Remember what I taught you about plants, sweet girl. They can heal or harm. Always choose to heal."

The vision shifted. Clara as a teenager, carefully tending a garden of medicinal herbs while jotting notes. Then Clara in her flower shop, scribbling in the book as she created arrangements to cheer up hospice patients. Each memory held in this treasured object showed Clara's deep connection to helping others through plants.

The vision released me, leaving me with absolute certainty: Clara might be fascinated by poisonous plants, but it appeared that she used her knowledge to heal, not harm.

"Your grandmother," I said softly. "She taught you about herbs."

Clara's eyes filled with tears. "Yes. How did you…?"

"I saw her giving you this notebook. And I saw how you've honored her legacy."

She took back the notebook, clutching it to her chest. "I would never use my knowledge to hurt anyone. It would betray everything she taught me."

After she slipped the notebook into her purse, she pulled out a delicate cotton handkerchief with a black smudge on the edge. "Here's something else. I used this in the downstairs bathroom while everyone was in the library, before Nico was in there and collapsed. My mascara was running because, you know, I can't seem to stop crying at anything. Even the coffee commercials make me cry these days. You know, the ones with the elderly couple who wakes up and drinks coffee in the morning mist?"

I nodded. The moment my fingers touched the damp fabric, another vision washed over me: Clara standing at the sink in the inn's downstairs bathroom, dabbing at her eyes with this very scrap of cloth. Through the bathroom window, lightning illuminated her tear-streaked face. She checked her phone while holding the handkerchief.

7:15 PM, about a half hour before Nico's collapse. The vision was perfectly clear: Clara had been nowhere near the kitchen. And she'd been with me in the library from the time Nico had walked in to give his speech. There were some gaps, but not many.

"You were in the bathroom around 7:15?" I asked.

Clara's jaw dropped. "Yes, exactly. How did you...? That's incredible. I remember hearing Nico shouting about his 'artistic vision' while I was in there."

Another piece clicked into place.

Thunder boomed again. I reached into my pocket and pulled out the green crystal, flashing it to Clara for a few seconds. "Now I have something to show you. I found this in Nico's hand after he died. When I touched it, I had a vision of you in the Astral Attic. With the toxic plant samples."

Clara leaned in, her voice barely audible. "They aren't shavings, they're for research. I bought them along with the crystals. They're actually seeds, and the sales clerk at the Astral Attic only would sell microscopic amounts. I'm scheduled to do a workshop series in Tampa on the dark history of common garden plants. You know, stuff like how Victorian women used foxglove in their gardens as both decoration and, well, for other purposes. The history fascinates me, probably because of my dad being a detective. But I'd never actually—" She broke off, apparently realizing how this sounded. "Oh my. You thought I killed Nico?"

"I... I'm sorry. I don't know what's up or down right now." I grimaced.

Until this moment, I'd never wondered what would happen if my psychic power had been of a different flavor. Now I wished I could read people's minds or magically discern the truth. Clara seemed like she was being honest, though. I could feel it in every cell in my body.

"I'd never kill anyone, especially not Nico," she whispered, a look of disgust crossing her face. "Who'd want to risk life in prison and the possibility of never drinking coffee or wine again for *that guy*? Did I just say that aloud? I'm sorry. Normally I'm a nice person."

I snickered despite myself. "You have a point. And if you were the killer, I doubt you'd be sitting here calmly discussing Victorian murder methods."

She frowned. Her next words were so quiet I had to strain to hear them. "It's one of my crystals. The green fluorite. I bought it because the woman at the shop said it was good for when life felt out of control."

"She wasn't wrong," I muttered.

"But how did Nico...?" She reached for it under the table, her fingers trembling. "I swear I had it in my purse when I came downstairs."

I scooted even closer to Clara. "I believe you," I whispered against her ear. "Something else is happening here. Mitzi's fountain pen is missing too, and my consecrated salt. Also a vintage lighter. Someone's collecting objects, and somehow Nico was involved."

Clara reached for her wine and tapped her fingernails against the glass. "You know, this reminds me of a case I heard about. The Hartley House murders in Vermont. The killer stole items of spiritual significance from each victim before..." She caught herself as Adam turned from the window. We both gave him a "oh this is such a sad situation" smile until he looked away.

I focused again on Clara. "That's interesting. Tell me more."

"It was on the 'Dark History of New England' podcast. A con man in 1987 targeted wealthy women who were into the occult. He'd steal their ritual objects. Crystals, pendulums, ritual jewelry. The theory was he was using them in spells to disorient his victims."

She took another sip of wine. "But here's where it gets interesting. Police never proved exactly what happened. Some thought he was working alone, others thought he had help. And when he died suddenly during a séance, there were three main theories: someone stopped him, he accidentally poisoned himself with his own concoction, or one of his victims finally got revenge."

I thought about Mitzi's increasingly erratic behavior. About that strange blue cocktail. About Ben's nervous energy all evening.

"In this case," I whispered, "someone might be collecting

mystical objects. But we don't know if Nico was the thief or if he merely got in the way."

Clara set down her glass. "Could be either. Or maybe someone in this room had a completely different reason to want him dead. Jealousy. Revenge. Greed. Those are the common ones. It's obvious the guy upset people simply with his terrible personality. Then there are things like mental illness, a crime of passion, and power. Could be any of them in this case. Or a combination. That's what I've learned in my years as a true crime lover."

She lifted her shoulders into a shrug. "But what do I know? I'm only a florist."

I held up my hands in a *stop* gesture. "And I'm only an innkeeper, but I've still solved murders. So don't say that. You know a lot. Maybe more than I do. I need your expertise and I think we can team up." My heartbeat kicked in. "Right now, we have a dead man in the kitchen, a storm outside, no phones, no cops, and someone in this room who's stealing magical objects and might have killed Nico."

Another bolt outside flashed, illuminating Clara's face. She leaned in, her eyes fierce. "Where do we start?"

Fifteen

After a quick discussion, we decided to leave Kristan, Ben, Adam, and the newlyweds in the dining room. They were behaving, and seemed to be appreciative when I brought in some bottled water and a few coffee table books, and tuned my battery-powered radio to WBOO. The local station was broadcasting weather updates and moody jazz, which seemed to lull them into a welcome silence, along with Kristan's steely, cool glances at everyone.

While toting votive candles, Clara and I marched into the library and found Jenny slouched sideways in an armchair. Mitzi was sprawled across my leather Chesterfield sofa. The council-woman's designer dress had ridden up to a scandalous height, and her expensive shoes lay scattered on my Persian rug.

Jenny looked up from her phone, which cast a blue glow over her worried face. "Still no signal, but I'm playing solitaire," she murmured, then gestured to the sleeping woman. "And she's been making these weird noises."

As if on cue, Mitzi let out a sound somewhere between a snore and a giggle.

"Has she been coherent at all?" I asked.

"Define coherent." Jenny sat up. "She tried to teach me the Electric Slide, then told me a twenty-minute story about the ghost of her first boyfriend's mother. Then she passed out mid-sentence while explaining why flip-flops are an affront to fashion."

Clara moved closer to Mitzi, her brow furrowed. "How quickly did that happen? The transition from dancing and talking to passing out?"

"Pretty fast," Jenny said. "I thought it was the wine, but..."

"But what?" I asked.

"Her behavior changed so suddenly."

"Hmm." The space between Clara's brows formed deep lines. "Like Nico."

Jenny nodded. "That."

"He was fine one moment, then, boom." Clara knelt beside the sofa. "I've heard about cases where toxins presented like extreme drunkenness. Maybe we should be worried."

Jenny surveyed the slumbering Mitzi. "Oh no. Should we try to make her throw up or something?"

"Let me check a few things first." Clara leaned closer to Mitzi, gently lifting one eyelid. "Her pupils are normal. Breathing is regular, if a bit snore-y. Pulse is strong but slow." She sat back on her heels and looked up at Jenny and me. "How much wine did she actually drink?"

"I lost count," Jenny admitted.

"I did, too," I said. "But she kept refilling from that bottle of red that Adam brought. The expensive one."

"The Château Margaux?" Clara raised an eyebrow. "That's a serious wine. And she was drinking it like fruit punch."

"While doing the Macarena," I added.

Mitzi shifted in her sleep, mumbling something about ghosts again.

"Is that her purse?" Clara pointed at an expensive, quilted black leather bag with the trademark Chanel C on the front. I nodded.

Clara reached for it and peered inside. "Aha."

She pulled out three small bottles of vodka, the kind you get on airplanes. "Can you, ah, read anything from these? Like when she drank them?"

I touched the small bottles one by one. The vision hit immediately: Mitzi in her BMW, parked in my lot outside. She was wearing the exact outfit she was in now, and the radio was on, tuned to a yacht rock station that mentioned the impending storm. She easily tossed back each miniature bottle of vodka, stuffed the empties in her purse, then checked her lipstick in the rearview mirror.

I handed the bottles back to Clara.

"Well," I sighed, "mystery solved. She pre-gamed in the parking lot. These were empty before she even came inside." I set the bottles on a side table. "The wine finished what the vodka started."

"Pre-gamed?" Clara looked confused. "Like tailgating?"

"It's what the kids call drinking before an event," Jenny explained, then added, "not that I would know anything about that."

I shot her a look, but now wasn't the time for a maternal lecture about college drinking. "I doubt she was poisoned with anything but alcohol. Though I wonder why a city council member would..."

"Show up to a fancy dinner already three sheets to the wind?" Clara finished. She was rifling through Mitzi's purse again. "Oh. Found some possible context." She held up a crumpled sheet of coffee-stained paper. "This is from a periodontist. She needs gum surgery and a root canal. Not just one. Three of them. And it's going to cost as much as a down payment on a house and her insurance won't pay."

Mitzi let out another snore-giggle and muttered something about groping Sean Connery. The three of us recoiled.

"That explains everything," I said softly. "Poor thing. I'll bet she's had a rough week."

Clara shoved the purse near Mitzi's bare feet then stood. "I think we can rule out poison. Some of the symptoms of certain plant-based toxins can look similar to extreme intoxication. But usually there would be—"

Mitzi suddenly sat bolt upright, eyes still closed, and announced: "That shirtless chef is tasty!" Then she flopped back down, snoring again.

We all stared at her. The corners of Jenny's mouth pulled back into a grimace.

"Yeah," Clara said finally. "That's wine, no question about it. Plus her breath is making the room smell like a vineyard."

I cringed. "Well, that's one less thing to worry about. Though we should probably get some water into her."

"Already tried," Jenny said. "She kept insisting it would 'dilute her spiritual connection to the other side.'"

Another crash of thunder made us all twitch. In the flash of lightning that followed, I spotted Jenny studying Clara with careful eyes.

"Sweetheart," I said softly, "there's something you need to know about Clara. She's not the killer."

"I knew it," Jenny said. "The true crime podcast thing threw you off, but like I said, most women are into that stuff. It's like a survival skill." She paused. "Though I still want to know how you're so sure Clara's Gucci."

"Hunh?" Clara and I both grunted. Why was my daughter talking about designer handbags at a time like this?

"Gucci. It means, good, cool," my daughter explained.

"I feel like I'm a million years old," I sighed. "Anyway. Here's how I know Clara is *Gucci*."

Clara's eyes shifted between the two of us, and I reached out and touched her arm, as if to say, *stay with me while I explain more weird stuff.*

I held up the green fluorite crystal that I'd found in Nico's hand. "Remember how I went into that trance earlier? Well, when I touched this, I saw Clara buying poisonous herbs at the Astral Attic. But then I touched her grandmother's notebook and saw something else entirely." I glanced at Clara. "Want to tell her, or should I?"

Clara smiled softly. "My grandmother taught me about plants. About healing. The toxic herbs were seeds, for research, for a workshop I'm planning. I'd never actually use them to harm anyone."

"Mom's good at reading people," Jenny said. "Even without the psychometry thing. Though I still think that's weird and I'm not sure I entirely believe it, but it seems solid. At least right now."

My heart ached, thinking of her trying to process all of this. First the experiences in Sedona, now a murder in her mother's home — the place she'd fled to because she wasn't feeling safe. I wanted to wrap her in my arms like when she was little, to protect her from both earthly and otherworldly dangers. But she wasn't a child anymore, and I couldn't shield her from everything, no matter how much I wanted to.

The rain beat on the windows. Mitzi mumbled something about dancing with Mick Jagger at Studio 54.

"Anyway. I think it's best that Clara help us," I said. "Maybe she should take a run at Adam and see if she can get info, since she's a stranger. And you and I," I touched Jenny's shoulder, "should try chatting with the newlyweds and Ben."

"Okay. But we should probably move her somewhere safer." Clara gestured to Mitzi. "We can't leave her passed out in here."

"Good point." I chewed my lip. "What if we put her in the bedroom with Freddie?"

"With my stuff? With your stuff?" Jenny yelped.

I winced, thinking of all the clothes spread around my bedroom. "Okay, how about in a guest room upstairs? There are three rooms open. The ones I prepped for Nico and his crew."

"Yes, excellent," Clara said. Jenny nodded.

"But we can't drag her upstairs in the dark," I said. "Hang on."

Carrying the little votive candle, I hurried to the front desk, using my phone's flashlight to navigate. In the bottom drawer, beneath a stack of tourist maps and brochures for ghost tours, I found Jimbo's emergency stash: a box of four LED headlamps he'd bought after our last power outage. He'd insisted we needed them "in case of a dire situation."

This seemed to fit that description. I tested one. It didn't work. I heaved a sigh then tried the others.

"Oh, thank goodness," I muttered as each illuminated brightly. I grabbed them and returned to the library.

I distributed the headlamps to Jenny and Clara. We strapped them on, adjusting the elastic bands. We all looked at each other and grinned. Here we were, in our cute dresses, wearing headlamps.

"We look like we're about to go spelunking," Jenny said, rolling her head around so the beam from her lamp whizzed around on the wall.

"Don't do that," I chided her. "It's making me queasy."

"So much for my hair. It looked terrible anyway," Clara said while looking at herself in a gilt-framed antique mirror on one wall.

"It did not," I countered. "You looked gorgeous."

Getting Mitzi upstairs proved to be an adventure in itself. She was almost entirely dead weight, and between shuffling and mumbling she kept sliding through our grip like a well-dressed jellyfish. The three of us struggled to guide her up the grand staircase while the storm raged outside. At one point we almost lost our hold on her, and I thought she'd tumble down the stairs.

Our headlamps cast jumping shadows on the walls.

"Left," I wheezed. "No, your other left, Jenny."

"Mom, she's heavier than she looks," Jenny grunted. "And I know what I'm doing. I've been to more than one frat party."

"I don't want to know," I said through gritted teeth.

Clara had Mitzi's feet, her headlamp beam bouncing off Mitzi's bare legs. "At least she's wearing nice underwear."

"Not looking," Jenny and I said in unison.

We finally managed to wrangle Mitzi into room 204 and onto the queen-sized bed. She immediately spread out like a starfish and resumed snoring.

"Whew. Hopefully we've solved *that* problem." I pressed my palm to my cheek. I was sweating. The elastic band of the head-lamp was already starting to itch on my forehead.

"Wait, what's that?" Clara said, her light beam catching something near the window. "Whose bag is that?"

A black duffel sat on the floor near the window. The curtains were open, and all we could see was rain streaking down the glass, and darkness beyond.

"Either Nico or Ben's. I cleaned this room earlier after last night's guest checked out. Ben probably brought it up earlier when I gave him the room keys."

We approached the duffel cautiously. It was expensive-looking leather with brass hardware that gleamed in the intersecting beams of our headlamps.

"Should we?" Jenny whispered, her light playing across the zipper as she moved her head this way and that.

I nodded. "Given the circumstances, I think we have to."

Clara picked it up and set it on an ottoman. All of us knelt on the floor, around the bag.

I unzipped it slowly, our three lights converging on its contents. Clara flipped a luggage tag on the handle. "This is definitely Nico's bag. See? It has his name and address."

Inside, next to some Axe body spray and nestled in a T-shirt, was something that made my breath catch: my jar of consecrated salt.

It had been wrapped carefully, cushioned and arranged with almost obsessive precision, a contrast to the chaos of Nico's other belongings strewn in the bag. It was as if two different people had packed this bag.

My hand went to another, similarly rolled up T-shirt. Inside was an expensive Mountblanc fountain pen. Clara grabbed another tightly packed shirt and unrolled the fabric.

The item inside glinted in the light of our headlamps: a silver Zippo lighter etched with the words YOU LIGHT UP MY LIFE, along with a bad portrait of Debbie Boone's face. "This your missing lighter?"

"Yes, it is," I said grimly. "It was my aunt's."

"Who's Debbie Boone?" Jenny asked while squinting.

"I'll explain later," I responded, grabbing another rolled up shirt. I unfurled it and a second green crystal rolled out. It twinkled in our lights and threw tiny, verdant refractions across the room. A few others followed.

"These are mine," Clara gasped, reaching for a thin, pale pink crystal with two pointy tips. "They're the ones I bought downtown today. Why are they in here? Why did Nico hold one as he was dying?"

"What the what," Jenny breathed.

"This might solve a few mysteries." I lifted Mitzi's fountain pen and inspected it. The thing looked expensive. I set it down and grabbed my jar of salt.

I touched each item several times, gently, hoping for a vision, but nothing came. Maybe I was too tired, or maybe the storm was interfering with my abilities. Who knew? I passed the objects to Clara, who in turn handed them to Jenny.

Clara handed me her crystal. I had a brief flicker of a cozy vision, of her buying it at the Astral Attic, along with the herb seeds. Sometimes my visions were like this — faint, pleasant snippets of something that happened in the past. I forced myself to snap out of the scene.

My eyes focused on Jenny, who was studying me with a skeptical face.

"I'm ok," I said, anticipating her question. Right now, I didn't want to get bogged down in explaining more about my abilities. Not when other, more pressing matters were at hand.

"It sure seems like Nico stole all this stuff," I said.

"But why? Why would he take these things? And when did he take them?" Jenny asked, her headlamp beam dancing across the duffel's contents. "I mean, the pen looks expensive, but that jar of salt? And some random crystals?"

Clara leaned closer. "In my true crime podcasts, thieves usually have clear motives. Money, revenge, obsession. But this seems random. And he could've stolen them at any time. Things were pretty chaotic downstairs for a while before he collapsed." She carefully moved aside a stack of tight black t-shirts and peered inside. "Unless there's something special about these items?"

I hesitated. How much should I explain about the magical properties of consecrated salt? Crystals and pens also had significance, as did vessels of fire. I was beginning to think our chef had some other ambitions that didn't include food.

"The salt is special to me," I said simply, not wanting to alarm anyone with my theories just yet. "And Mitzi seemed pretty upset about losing that pen earlier."

"Wait, what's this?" Jenny asked.

She pulled out a phone in a sleek, black case.

"It might be Nico's personal phone," I said. "Ben was carrying the ones they used for filming. I didn't see Nico on a phone at all, except for when we arrived and he was talking in the driveway."

"And look," Jenny murmured, pressing the home button. The screen lit up, no password required. "Who doesn't lock their phone these days?"

"Someone who's overly confident," Clara murmured. "Or stupid."

I glanced at the snoring Mitzi, then back at the glowing screen. I nodded in Jenny's direction, the light of my headlamp bobbing.

Jenny's finger hovered over the screen. "Where do we start? Messages? Social media? Email?"

"Whatever feels right to you. While you go through the phone, Clara and I will look through the rest of the bag."

Jenny glanced at me, her face scrunched up in a frown. "Should we be worried about, like, fingerprints?"

I shook my head. "I'll tell the cops we were searching in his stuff for an emergency contact."

Jenny swallowed. "You answered that way too quick, Mom, and with a lot of confidence."

"This isn't my first rodeo," I said grimly while plunging my hand into a side pocket of the duffel.

Shaking her head, Jenny sat back against the wall, flicked off her headlamp, and focused intently on the cellphone like the Gen Z kid she was.

Meanwhile Clara was busy pulling every item in the duffel out and placing it on the floor in a semi-circle around us. In addition to the stolen mystical objects, the contents painted a perfect picture of Nico's personality: a total of three types of Axe body spray, a bamboo matcha set still in its box, expensive hair products, a stack of black boxer briefs, a leather vest, and a selfie ring light. Also a box of condoms, which made me wince.

There was also a protein powder container, a pair of fingerless leather gloves, and—most telling of all—a framed photo of himself shirtless in what appeared to be a professional kitchen.

"This all seems normal," I said to Clara. "Ridiculous but normal."

"Holy crap," Jenny stretched her leg out and nudged me with her sandaled foot and switched on her headlamp. "Mom. Clara. You need to see this."

She turned the screen toward us. Clara and I huddled together as we read.

It was a Notes app entry, dated today, titled "Crescent Moon Dinner." Below it was a list of everyone in the house along with some disturbing observations.

Mitzi Blackwood: City council, married, major gambling debts - useful

Marc & Sarah Anderson: Honeymooners, trust fund babies - useful

Kristan Jones: Chamber of Commerce connections - useful

Adam Stone: Horrible, knows too much - disposable
Amelia Matthews: Divorced inn owner, thinks she's a witch,
wears hippie dresses - disposable
Jenny Matthews: daughter of Amelia - smokin' hot
Clara Whitman: Last-minute addition - unknown

"He called my baby *what*?" My voice came out as a growl. "I'm going to kill him again."

I sat back on my heels, my mind swimming with anger and this new information. The collection of mystical objects troubled me deeply, as did Nico's note.

Each item held power in its own way. Back in California, I would have scoffed at such a notion. But Cypress Grove had taught me that seemingly ordinary objects could hold extraordinary energy. Especially my consecrated salt.

Was Nico collecting them for some ritual? Or had he simply been like a crow, drawn to stealing shiny objects? He certainly hadn't struck me as someone with any understanding of magic. Even his blue cocktail was likely more theater than substance, although I would've liked to know what was really in the glass.

Mitzi let out another thunderous snore, and I idly wondered if she'd ever been assessed for sleep apnea. Jenny's headlamp beam swung toward the bed, then back to the duffel bag.

"Mom," she whispered, "What I don't understand is why Nico labeled some people as 'useful' and others as 'disposable.' What was he planning?"

"And why mark me as 'unknown?'" Clara added. "Though I suppose showing up last minute threw a wrench in whatever he was plotting."

I touched the crystal in my pocket, but no new visions came. Sometimes psychometry was like that, offering glimpses of truth when I least expected, then going quiet when I needed it most.

Like many things about my new life, I was still learning its rhythms.

"Whatever his plan was," I said firmly, "it died with him.

Right now we need to focus on finding out who killed him and keeping everyone safe until help arrives." I gave Jenny's arm a reassuring squeeze.

Clara nodded. "The three of us have to stick together."

Jenny started to protest, but something in my expression made her stop. Instead, she helped Clara carefully repack the duffel bag. As she did, I noticed her hands were steady, even as mine trembled slightly. Why did that both terrify and fill me with pride?

Mitzi let out an incoherent babble, and somewhere upstairs, a door slammed, making us all jump.

All three of our headlamp beams swung toward the bedroom door. Footsteps on the hardwood floor of the hallway, getting closer. Purposeful ones. Not the tentative steps of someone navigating in the dark, but the confident stride of someone who knew exactly where they were going.

And it sounded as if they were heading straight for us.

Sixteen

We froze at the sound of footsteps coming down the hall. We finished stuffing everything back into the duffel while our head-lamp beams bounced wildly around the room.

"Quick," I whispered, shoving the bag to Jenny, who was closest to the bed. "under there."

Jenny slid it beneath the antique four-poster just as we heard a hesitant knock at the door. Mitzi let out another chainsaw-like snore.

"Hello?" a male voice called. "Uh. Amelia? Are you up here?"

I recognized Marc Anderson's voice and let out a breath. "Yes, come in!"

The door opened and Marc's confused face appeared, illuminated by the glow of his phone flashlight. He blinked at our head-lamps. "Oh, wow, those are smart. Where'd you get them?"

"Employee emergency kit," I said, trying to act as though sitting on the floor, in the dark, while wearing a headlamp, was totally normal. "What's up?"

"We, uh." He glanced at Mitzi's sprawled form. "Whoa. Is she okay?"

"She's fine," Clara said smoothly. "Taking a little rest. The evening's events were a bit much for her."

Marc nodded. "Yeah, about that. We were all kind of freaking out downstairs. Kristan has some movie downloaded on her tablet. Something with Meryl Streep singing ABBA songs? She thought it might help everyone calm down. But we need pillows and blankets so we can camp out in the parlor or whatever that room with the witch altar is called."

Jenny's headlamp beam swung toward me. "Mamma Mia? Really? I love that movie!"

I shot her a look that said, *no way, kiddo*. She clammed up.

"Better than sitting around thinking about..." Marc's voice trailed off and he swallowed hard.

"Of course," I said quickly. "Jenny, Clara, can you stay with Mitzi, while I help Marc?"

They nodded, though I was aware of Jenny's worried expression. I touched her arm as I passed. "It's fine," I whispered. "You're safe with Clara."

I climbed to my feet and led Marc into the hallway, my headlamp illuminating the way. "The linen closet is right down here," I said, trying to sound casual. "Though I should warn you, it might be a little haunted."

"A little?"

"I've heard some things coming from this closet in the past." I paused at the closet door. "Unusual noises. Never have seen anything, but I want you to be prepared."

Marc stared at me. "I honestly can't tell if you're pulling my leg."

I smiled and opened the door, though I couldn't help glancing around. I wasn't joking; occasionally I'd heard strange noises coming from this upstairs closet. I'd told myself that it was a mouse, or a Florida gecko. But while I hadn't seen any hard evidence of a supernatural being, I also wasn't totally convinced the noises were of this earthly plane.

Frankly, I'd been a tad too busy over the past few months to really pay much attention.

As long as the spirit or whatever stayed in here, mostly silent, everything was cool. We could coexist peacefully. If middle age had taught me anything, it was that I couldn't do it all.

The closet was in its pristine, organized state, just as I'd left it. Sweet. I reached for a pillow. "Anyway, Marc. You and Sarah seem to be handling all this pretty well."

He helped me gather an armload of blankets. "Are we? Because I feel like I'm in some weird dream. Or maybe a murder mystery dinner theater gone wrong." He let out a shaky laugh. "Sarah's the one holding it together. She keeps saying it's like a Lifetime movie, but with real people who smell funny."

He paused. "Not you, of course. You smell fine. She meant that Nico guy. Man, he really pours on the Axe body spray. Sarah's really sensitive to cologne."

Lightning flashed through the window at the end of the hall, followed by immediate thunder.

"Had you ever met Nico before tonight?" I asked, trying to sound casual while handing him a stack of pillows.

"No, thankfully." Marc shifted the blankets in his arms. "Sarah's the one who wanted to come to this dinner. She follows him on TikTok. Or followed him, I guess." He winced. "Sorry, that was insensitive."

"It's fine." I grabbed more pillows. "So you didn't know anything about him? His background, his career?"

"Only what Sarah told me. That he was some social media chef who got famous during the pandemic. She thought it would be fun to see him in person while we were staying here." He shrugged. "We've been having such a great time at the inn, exploring the town. And exploring Florida. It's all been great. This whole town is fun. Well, except for tonight."

I assessed him in the beam of my headlamp. His earnest face, his rumpled polo shirt, the way he carefully cradled the blankets like they were precious cargo. Either Marc Anderson was an Oscar-worthy actor, or he was exactly what he appeared to be: a Midwest newlywed caught up in something way over his head.

"One more thing," I said as we slowly headed downstairs, our steps illuminated only by my headlamp. "Did you happen to notice anything strange about Nico's behavior tonight? Before he, you know." I couldn't finish the sentence.

"You mean besides the fact that he wasn't wearing a shirt?" Marc snorted. "The guy seemed like a total tool. Sorry, I know he's dead and all, but wow. Sarah's already deleted his TikTok account from her following list. She said she can't believe she ever thought his videos were interesting. She thinks he's a jerk. Was a jerk."

We reached the bottom of the stairs, where I could hear Kristan's tablet playing what sounded like "Dancing Queen."

"The only weird thing," Marc added, "was how he kept going through everyone's stuff when they weren't looking. I saw him rifling through a purse right before cocktail hour. I was going to say something but you looked overwhelmed and I thought maybe it was his man bag."

I nearly stumbled. "He what?"

"Yeah, it was strange. I figured he was looking for his phone or something. I tried to tell that Ben guy but he got a phone call." Marc shrugged. "Anyway, thanks for the blankets. You coming to watch the movie?"

I shook my head, and out of the corner of my eye, I saw his wife, Sarah, in the dining room.

"Marc, why don't you get everyone settled? I noticed Sarah's in the dining room and I'd like a quick word with her, to make sure she's holding up. I'm worried about everyone."

He balanced the stack of bedding in both arms. "Sure. I bet she's fussing over the table. She likes to clean when she's anxious, and I always join her so she's not alone. But I'll hold off this time." His little smile told me volumes about their relationship.

Marc headed into the parlor and I power walked to the dining room, where Sarah was trying to scoop a crumbled cracker off the tablecloth. In the dim light from the votives, Sarah looked young and vulnerable.

"You don't need to do all this," I said softly.

She startled. "Oh! Hi Amelia. I couldn't leave it like this." She gestured at the chaos.

"Really, it's okay. I'll get it all later tonight, or tomorrow." I shuddered to think what the inn would look like tomorrow, both literally and metaphorically.

Sarah's hands shook slightly as she righted a wine glass. "This isn't how I imagined tonight would go. When I saw Nico was the chef, I was so excited. I'd watched all his videos." She gave a bitter laugh. "Guess you can't trust what you see online."

"No?" I kept my voice neutral, reaching for a cracker that was still in cellophane.

"He was so different in person. Cruel. The way he treated Ben, my gosh." She shook her head. "I deleted Nico's account. I feel stupid for ever being a fan."

"That's not stupid. We all want to believe in people." I paused, then asked casually while gesturing with the cracker, "Did you interact with Nico much tonight? Before everything happened?"

"No, thank goodness. I couldn't believe how he acted, though." She wrapped her arms around herself. "I can't believe he's dead. I mean, I didn't like him, but no one deserves that."

"It's okay to have complicated feelings about this."

She nodded, then glanced in the direction of the door, where a muffled song was playing.

"You should go watch the movie," I said. "Try to take your mind off all this. I'm sure the police will be here soon."

She nodded and whispered a thanks before scampering off.

I clambered up the stairs while munching on the cracker, my mind racing. Sarah definitely didn't seem like a suspect, and neither did her husband. Neither had motive, in my opinion.

But something nagged at me about Ben and Nico. Why hadn't anyone observed anything about Ben? Had they been working together somehow? Ben helping Nico steal things in exchange for... what? That didn't track though. Ben seemed terrified of Nico, and Nico treated him like dirt.

I burst back into room 204, where Clara and Jenny were sitting on a loveseat, their headlamp beams aimed straight ahead on the duffel bag, which was now on the floor. Jenny had Nico's phone in her hand. Mitzi was still snoring, though now she'd somehow managed to wrap herself in the duvet like a burrito.

"Mom!" Jenny looked up. "What happened?"

"Well, Marc saw Nico going through a purse right before cocktail hour." The two of them scooted over and we all crowded on the tiny sofa. "Sounds like he was definitely stealing things, and …"

Clara nodded. "That fits with what we found in his bag. But why? What's the connection between a fountain pen, some crystals, and consecrated salt?"

"Maybe he was building some kind of collection?" Jenny suggested.

"Or maybe he thought they had monetary value," I said, though something nagged at me about that theory. "Let's talk about the people downstairs who had reason to kill him. I don't think it was Marc, honestly. He seems too…"

"Clueless?" Jenny chimed in.

"Yeah," I said.

Jenny sighed. "Okay, so we have Sarah Anderson, Kristan from the Chamber, Adam the wine guy, and Ben the assistant."

"What about Sarah?" Clara asked. "She seems sweet, but sometimes the quiet ones…"

"No," Jenny said firmly. "When Nico was making that gross blue cocktail, Sarah was in the bathroom. I know because she was coming out of the bathroom as I was going in, and we had this whole conversation about your hand soap and where to buy it." She looked up from her phone. "That was right before everything happened."

"Yeah, and I chatted with Sarah briefly downstairs. I really don't think she did it," I said. "Plus Marc said she was a fan of Nico's videos. Both she and Marc seem far too normal to commit murder. They have zero motive."

Clara and Jenny both nodded, the lights on their foreheads bouncing and creating a disco-like effect in the room.

"That leaves us with Kristan, Adam, and Ben," Jenny said, ticking them off on her fingers.

"Kristan organized this whole thing," I said slowly. "But why would she want to kill the star attraction? Clara, you know her from college, right? Is she capable of something like this? That doesn't make sense, though. Then again, nothing does, not tonight."

"Yeah, we were sorority sisters at UMass," Clara said, adjusting her headlamp so the beam pointed straight up, toward the ceiling. "She was my rock during, well, during a really bad time."

Jenny and I waited while Clara gathered her thoughts.

"My freshman year, there was this guy. A teaching assistant in my botany class. He was charming, brilliant. Started giving me special attention, telling me I had talent." Clara's voice got tight. "Then he began stalking me. Notes in my mailbox. Showing up wherever I went. It got really scary."

"Oh Clara," I breathed.

My daughter's expression tightened.

"Kristan figured out what was happening before I did. She helped me document everything, got campus security involved. When he finally confronted me one night after class..." Clara swallowed hard. "Kristan was there. She'd been following me, keeping watch. She pepper-sprayed him, called the cops. Testified at his disciplinary hearing."

"That's intense," Jenny whispered.

Clara nodded. "After that, Kristan became almost obsessed with protecting other women. She organized safety workshops, started a buddy system for late-night study groups. She's the most protective person I know." She looked up at us. "That's why, when my marriage fell apart and I needed somewhere safe to start over, she suggested Florida. Suggested Cypress Grove and Sunny Shores. I chose the latter because it's known for being a tropical plant mecca. She said it was a place where women looked out for each other."

"So she wouldn't have brought Nico here if she thought he was dangerous," I said slowly.

"No way. She vets everyone. Thoroughly." Clara twisted her hands in her lap. "Though she did seem stressed when I called last week. Not like herself. Kept talking about how this dinner series had to be perfect, how the Chamber was counting on her."

"But killing someone?" Jenny asked.

"Never." Clara's voice was firm. "Kristan's ambitious, but she fights for people, not against them. The worst thing she ever did in college was accidentally release a bunch of lab rats because she thought they were being mistreated. Then she spent three days helping to catch them all. It was a mess."

"Yes, and from what I know about her, I don't think she'd risk her career for a guy like Nico," I said.

"Definitely not," Clara said.

"So that leaves us with Adam and Ben," Jenny said, ticking off names on her fingers. "Adam clearly hated Nico."

"And Nico treated Ben like dirt," I said.

We sat in silence for a few minutes, absorbing everything.

"So what should we do?" Jenny finally said.

I turned to my daughter. "Did you see anything else in Nico's phone?"

She wrinkled her nose. "Several sexual texts to a bunch of women. So cringe. Want to hear them?"

I shut my eyes for a second. "Absolutely not unless they're relevant to our investigation."

"Wait," Jenny exclaimed, her fingers flying over Nico's phone. "Some of these texts are from today. Look at this exchange with Ben from this morning."

Clara and I leaned in close. "Who's texting what?"

"Ben's texts are on the left, Nico's on the right," Jenny said.

The fish delivery isn't right. This isn't what we ordered.

I switched suppliers. Better price.

Are you insane, Nico? You can't just switch fugu suppliers!

Stay in your lane, little man. Remember who signs your checks.

This isn't safe. You need proper certification for this.

I know what I'm doing, bro

No you don't. You're going to get someone killed.

Have you finished the social media calendar? I want to film at three at my house. Don't be late. I'm done with this conversation, Ben.

"Sus," Jenny said.

I figured that meant "suspect" in Gen Z speak.

"Well, that's troubling," Clara whispered.

"There's more from earlier this week," Jenny said, scrolling up. "Lots of Ben asking about the details of tonight's event. Mundane stuff. Nico brushed him off every time."

I sat back, my headlamp beam bouncing off the ceiling. "So Ben knew Nico was being reckless with the fugu."

"And now Nico's dead," Clara said softly.

We all looked at each other, our headlamp beams criss-crossing.

"We need to talk to both of them," I said. "Adam *and* Ben. Ben seems like the perfect suspect, but Adam's anger toward Nico can't be ignored either. He's normally a calm guy but the look I saw in his eyes tonight made me shiver, you know?"

Clara and Jenny nodded.

I continued. "Jenny, maybe you can chat up Kristan, that's safe enough. Clara, could you feel out Adam? See what he knows about Nico's restaurant history? He might open up to you since you don't know each other. I'll talk to Ben."

Clara nodded. "I can pretend to be interested in opening a wine bar in Sunny Shores. Get him talking about the industry."

"Perfect." I stood, my knees creaking. "Let's head downstairs."

In the back of my mind, I also wanted to chat with Kristan. It wasn't that I didn't trust Clara or her assessment of her friend; I merely wanted to cover all my bases.

Thunder crashed overhead, so close and loud it made the windows rattle in their frames. Through the warped Victorian glass, I could see sheets of rain falling sideways. The wind sure had picked up considerably since we'd come upstairs.

I began to wonder if this was some kind of freak hurricane, and not a routine summer storm. I'd never seen it rain so hard in my life, and I wondered if the inn's roof was sound. How old was the roof, anyway? I made a mental note to check the documents left behind by my aunt when this situation was all over.

Thoughts of dealing with an insurance claim and a roof repair seemed almost as daunting as a mysterious death.

When we reached the parlor, Pierce Brosnan was warbling on Kristan's tablet, Sarah and Marc were cuddled under a blanket, Ben sat alone in the corner fiddling with his phone tripod, and Kristan was scribbling furiously in a black leather notebook.

Adam was nowhere to be seen.

Seventeen

The three of us huddled in the doorway, taking in the scene.

"Hey, gang," I said in a friendly voice. Everyone tore their eyes away from the tablet. "Has anyone seen Adam?"

Marc shrugged. "I think he went to get more wine?"

"Or maybe a phone call, although I don't think the cell service is working yet," Sarah added vaguely. "I wasn't paying attention because we were reading the latest weather forecast. There are only a few more rain bands on the radar. But the flooding is bad near the Interstate."

"Good to know," I said.

Ben didn't look up or respond. Kristan grimaced and shrugged, as if to acknowledge that this entire evening was a lost cause.

I gave a little wave, which everyone ignored, then gestured for Jenny and Clara to follow me into the library. We huddled by the front desk, an old antique thing. Once we were out of earshot, our headlamp beams converged on the floor as we formed a tight circle.

"We need to find Adam," I whispered. "Where is he? Did he leave?"

"Super sus," Jenny muttered.

"Would he be stupid enough to leave in this weather?" Clara nodded at the front door, which was rattling with the wind.

"I don't even want to think about what that means if he left," I sighed. "So, change of plans. Instead of talking to everyone like we discussed, let's all look for Adam first."

"Excellent idea. We should set a time to meet back up, though," Clara said.

"If one of us doesn't meet back here in twenty, send a search party," Jenny added. She adjusted her headlamp. "Geez, this thing's itchy. I hope it doesn't leave a permanent mark on my forehead."

I brushed a lock of her silky hair out of her face. "It won't, sweetheart. A little facial massage will fix that. I know the owner of the best spa in town."

"A spa day?" Her face brightened. "That would be amazing. I mean, if we get through tonight."

"That does sound so good," Clara groaned. "But let's deal with this first."

My first instinct was to keep Jenny with me, to protect her. But then I remembered how she'd handled herself tonight. How she'd faced down mysterious lights in Sedona, managed a drunken Mitzi, and kept her cool through all of this. My daughter wasn't just capable; she was extraordinary.

"Jenny, you take the second floor," I said. "Look in all the rooms. Clara, can you check the dining room and front areas? I'll search the apartment." I hesitated. "Everyone meet back here in the lobby in twenty minutes. No matter what."

I checked my smart watch. Clara did the same. Jenny flicked her phone on.

"Are you sure about splitting up?" Clara asked. "It feels very much like a horror movie."

Thunder crashed, the wind howling through the eaves like a living thing.

"Jenny, are you okay with this? Maybe you should come with me," I said, a well of panic rising in my throat.

"We'll cover more ground this way," Jenny said. She touched my arm. "Mom, I've got this."

I couldn't help but smile. "When did you get so brave?"

"Probably around the time I started getting cosmic downloads from UFOs." She grinned, then grew serious. "Really, Mom. I'm okay. After what happened in Sedona, a missing wine guy and some thunder isn't going to freak me out."

Here was my daughter, who only yesterday had been horrified by my witch status, now cracking jokes about her own supernatural experiences. Maybe we weren't so different after all.

"Twenty minutes," I repeated. "And Jenny? Be careful. You too, Clara."

She nodded, already moving toward the stairs. "You too, Mom. Both of you."

Clara and I watched her go, our headlamp beams following her ascent until she disappeared onto the second floor.

"She's something, that's for sure," Clara murmured. "At her age I would've been freaking out. Or drinking heavily."

I sucked in a breath. "Yeah, me too. Probably both."

Clara headed toward the dining room, and I turned toward the kitchen, trying to ignore the knot in my stomach. The beam of my headlamp amplified the dust motes dancing in the air, and the inn felt different somehow. Darker. More ominous. Even the familiar creak of the floorboards under my feet seemed sinister.

I hated that almost as much as the fact that a man had been killed tonight. The Crescent Moon Inn had become my happy place, my solace, my source of serenity. Every day I woke up and tried to bring a slice of happiness to my guests, which in turn, filled my own well of joy.

How dare someone try to steal that from me? Especially while my daughter was here? A sense of indignancy bubbled up. Now I was determined to figure this out. Starting with Adam.

I pulled the bookcase door open to my apartment, wincing at how loud the hinges sounded in the silence. The living room was as I'd left it, still and dark. And yet, I knew there was another presence in my space, and it wasn't just the dead man in the kitchen.

I felt it in my bones.

Taking slow, soft steps, I moved toward the kitchen. I heard a muffled tap. A footstep? My heart rate spiked. I could now see Nico's feet, still uncovered on the floor. But was someone else in the kitchen? I couldn't see from this angle.

I probably should have armed myself with something. Crud. Well, I guess I had the element of surprise on my side.

I burst into the doorway.

There was a figure crouched beside Nico's, wearing yellow rubber gloves like the ones I kept under the sink for dishes.

It was Adam.

He looked up, squinting at my headlamp beam. "I can explain," he said quietly.

"You'd better." I kept my voice steady, though my heart felt like it was beating out of my chest. "And maybe start with why you're wearing my dish gloves."

"The gloves?" Adam glanced at his hands as if surprised to find them covered in yellow rubber. "Oh. Right. I found them under your sink. I didn't want to touch anything. I've watched enough true crime shows to know about evidence."

"So you wanted to dispose of evidence, you mean?"

"Look, before you jump to conclusions—"

"I'm way past jumping," I said, crossing my arms. "I'm so far past jumping I'm basically in orbit. Did you kill Nico?"

I hated acting like this with my friend. I liked the guy, I adored his wine bar, and admired his taste in California varietals. But I had to overlook all of that to find out the truth.

The words hung in the air between us. I tilted my chin down, pointing my head lamp directly in his face.

"No," he said finally. "I wanted to. God knows I had reason to. But I didn't."

I appraised him in the beam of my headlamp. His usually perfectly-styled hair was disheveled, like he'd been running his hands through it. His button-down was wrinkled, and his face had the haunted look of someone carrying a heavy burden. He slowly stood up and walked toward me.

"Tell me about what's going on with you two," I said, taking a step back.

He flinched. "Can you angle that light off my face?"

"Uh, I guess." I reached up and adjusted the headband.

Adam sighed and sank into one of my kitchen chairs. He was still wearing the rubber gloves. "It was seven years ago. Nico was young, not even twenty two, and worked at my first wine bar as a sommelier in training. I trained him myself. Taught him everything he knew about wine. He was charismatic. Good with customers. Too good, as it turned out."

I perched on the edge of the chair across from him. "Go on."

"Things started disappearing. Small stuff at first. Expensive bottles of wine. Cash from the register. Then customers started reporting missing items. A watch here, a piece of jewelry there. Always after private tastings that Nico conducted."

"He was stealing from your customers?"

Adam nodded grimly. "And that wasn't even the worst part. He'd take weird things. Personal items. One woman lost her grandmother's rosary. Another guy reported his lucky poker chip missing. And get this — my own mother's crystal gravy boat vanished after Nico did a private wine dinner at her house."

I thought of the objects we'd found in Nico's bag. The pattern was starting to make sense. Sort of.

"Did you confront him?"

"I did." Adam's normally upbeat voice took on a hollow quality. "He denied everything. Then one night, I caught him in the act. He was going through a customer's purse during a wine class." His hands clenched into fists, making the rubber gloves squeak against each other. The sound seemed to startle him again, as if he'd forgotten he was wearing them.

"Wow." I shook my head. "And what did he do?"

"He threatened to expose some creative accounting I'd done

when the bar was struggling. Said he'd make sure I lost my liquor license." Adam's laugh was bitter. "I'd given him access to everything. My books, my clients, my reputation. He played me perfectly."

I let that sink in. "So what happened?"

"He quit the next day. Disappeared. I heard rumors that he'd pulled similar stunts at other restaurants, other bars. Then he surfaced as an influencer on TikTok. He had his controversies there, too, but I ignored it all. I'd rebuilt my life and am in a good spot here in Cypress Grove. I met Jason, fell in love, and Grape Escape is thriving. Why would I throw all that away?"

"Hmm," I hummed, not knowing what to think. "Why didn't you bring Jason tonight?"

"Someone needed to stay with the puppy."

"Oh, right." My mind flashed back to earlier in the evening, when Adam had arrived. We'd discussed this, but those moments seemed like a decade ago, and not a few hours.

"I know it's difficult to believe, but I saw Nico on TikTok about six months ago and all I could do was laugh. I felt grateful that I'd left that part of my life behind. Even though it wasn't fair that he always managed to stay one step ahead of consequences." Adam gestured at Nico's covered form. "Until now, I guess."

I narrowed my eyes. "So if you put it all behind you, then why did you come tonight? To confront him? Prove that you're successful? Was it some male ego thing? That's what I don't get."

He shook his head vigorously. "No, I swear, Amelia. I didn't know he was going to be here. Kristan said she'd lined up some great chefs for the pop-ups. I didn't pay attention to who all was coming, and she made it seem like the first one would be a surprise celeb. So I paid to attend, thinking it would be fun and we could hang out and drink wine, all of us together."

"Really?" I was dubious. "You had no idea he'd be here?"

"None. When I saw him in your kitchen, shirtless and ridiculous..." Adam shuddered. "I almost left. But then I thought, why should I? I own a successful business. I have a wonderful partner.

A life I love. Why let him chase me away? This is my town, not his."

That tracked with what I knew of Adam. Still, I had to be thorough.

"Would you mind if I, uh." I cleared my throat. How to phrase this? I hadn't ever told Adam about my abilities. "Could I hold something of yours? Something you've had with you all evening?"

His brow furrowed and he folded down one cuff of his glove and scratched his wrist. "Like what? Why?"

"Your wallet maybe? Or that bracelet?" I pointed to the braided leather band on his bare wrist. "It's for my psychometry. I can sometimes see visions when I touch objects. To confirm your story."

"You're psychic?" His eyebrows shot up. "I had no idea."

"I don't advertise it." I shrugged. "It's relatively new. Since moving here."

"Huh." He nodded thoughtfully. "I wouldn't have pegged you for having abilities. You seem so..."

"Plain?" I asked, trying not to sound defensive.

"No, no. More like, grounded? You haven't made it your whole personality, like some folks in town. No offense to them, but sometimes it's a bit much with the flowing scarves and crystal healing amulets everywhere. I had a customer in the other day who insisted on saging the place before she ordered a glass of wine."

I had to laugh at that. "Well, I do own some scarves. And crystals. But I try to keep it low-key."

"Sure." He carefully peeled off one rubber glove and unclasped the bracelet. "Jason made this for me. Never take it off. Will it help?"

The moment the bracelet touched my palm, the vision hit: Adam sitting at the bar in Grape Escape, Jason fastening this very bracelet around his wrist, both of them laughing. Adam reached to cup Jason's cheek while thanking him. The scene was suffused with love and contentment.

Then another flash: Adam earlier this evening, gripping the kitchen counter as he watched Nico strut around. His knuckles were white, but he didn't move. Didn't act on his anger.

The vision released me, and I handed the bracelet back. "Thanks. What else do you have on you, something you've carried all night?"

"My watch?" He slipped off an expensive-looking Rolex. "I checked the time constantly tonight, wondering when this nightmare would end."

When my fingers closed around the watch face, a series of quick visions flashed through my mind: Adam at 7:10 PM, standing in my living room clutching a wine glass while Nico performed for the camera. Then Adam at 7:30, in the kitchen, arguing with Nico. Adam stalked out. The watch's second hand kept moving, marking each moment.

It sure seemed as though Adam was telling the truth.

I handed it back, and Adam dug in his pocket and pulled out what looked like a small metal bar with various buttons and rollers. "Try this. Been fiddling with this all night. Nervous habit. My therapist suggested it when I quit smoking last year."

I glanced at the thing. "What is it?"

"A fidget toy. Apparently it works better than nicotine gum. It's about keeping my hands busy."

"What will they think of next," I murmured, taking it into my hand.

The vision came immediately: 8:05 PM, Adam in the library during the chaos after Nico collapsed, pacing and clicking the metal switches. Then at 8:15, Adam in the parlor, standing far from the others, still working the cube's roller ball with his thumb while Mitzi began her drunken performance.

The visions confirmed it. Through the critical moments of the evening, Adam had been in full view of others, nowhere near the kitchen alone with Nico.

"Okay," I said, handing back the fidget thingamabob. "I believe you."

"That's fascinating." He rubbed his wrist where the bracelet usually sat. "Must be quite a gift. And burden."

"Sometimes both," I admitted. "Thanks for being understanding about it."

"Did you see—"

"Enough to know you're telling the truth." I glanced at my watch. Twenty minutes had flown by in no time, and I rose from my seat, and moved toward the door while averting my eyes from the (covered) body on the floor.

"Crud. I need to meet Jenny and Clara in the lobby. But Adam? You should probably get back to the others. When the cops get here it's going to look bad if people know you're in here."

"Yeah, you're probably right."

"Wait." I paused at the doorway and turned to look at Adam, who was setting the rubber gloves in the sink. "What were you looking for anyway? When I found you here?"

"Honestly? I was trying to make sense of the fugu thing." Adam shook his head, moving toward me. We walked out of the room together.

"What fugu thing?" I scowled.

"Nico never showed any interest in fish or Asian cuisine when I knew him. He was obsessed with wine, sure, and loved showing off. But this?" He gestured back at the kitchen and the now-smelly fish on the floor. "It's weird."

"Maybe fame changed him?" I suggested.

"Maybe. But something doesn't add up." He frowned. "The guy I knew couldn't tell a tuna roll from a unagi nigiri. Now suddenly he's a fugu expert? It's like..." He trailed off, clearly troubled, and shook his head.

"Here's what I don't get," I said, then explained about the missing items we found in Nico's bag. "Do you think Nico was stealing them for some ritual spell or supernatural purpose?"

Adam snorted a laugh. "No. He wouldn't know a spell from a sock. He was a garden-variety kleptomaniac."

"Interesting," I whispered. Things were coming into clearer focus. Sort of.

Adam and I left my apartment. I made sure the bookcase door was locked this time. Adam went left toward the parlor, and I made my way to the lobby. Three minutes until our meeting time.

My footsteps quickened as I approached the front desk. Clara was already there, her face flushed with excitement.

"Amelia," she whispered urgently. "You're not going to believe what I saw. And what I found."

Eighteen

Clara could barely stand still as we waited by the front desk for Jenny. Her face was flushed with excitement, and she kept shifting from foot to foot.

"What did you find? Tell me," I whispered.

"Let's wait for Jenny. You both need to hear this."

She was right. The three of us were a team. "Okay. I have some news too."

The storm continued its assault on the inn, and I wondered if the old Victorian windows could withstand this much rain. My headlamp beam zeroed in on Jenny hurrying down the stairs, and Clara practically vibrated with the need to share her discovery.

"Hey," Jenny asked, joining our huddle by the desk. "How'd you do? I found some wild stuff."

"So did we." I reached to squeeze my daughter's upper arm, feeling the need to touch my baby. "Clara first."

Clara's eyes were wide with fear. "I was checking upstairs like we planned, and saw Ben slip into that old half bath in the hall. I guess it's unused?"

I shook my head. "I store extra toiletries there. The door is sticky and the toilet's a bit wonky."

Clara continued. "I hid behind that big statue of a man in the hall. The one with the hand on his hip. He looks creepy."

"Oh, that's John Gorrie. He was a Floridian who invented air conditioning. My aunt bought it years ago. Apparently she thought he was a true hero," I said.

Jenny mopped her brow. "Eternal shoutout to that guy."

A flash of exasperation crossed Clara's face. "Anyway. There was a crack in the bathroom door and I could barely see Ben. I mean, I wasn't trying to spy on him while he was doing his business but I knew something was up because of the odor. He was burning something. Paper. I could smell it."

She pulled a charred, limp scrap from her pocket with trembling fingers. "I made a scratching noise on the wall to interrupt him. He heard and flushed the toilet—"

"Wait," I interrupted her. "There's a sign that says, 'do not flush.'"

"Mom, I don't think people are following rules tonight."

"Right." I frowned, wondering if I had a plumbing crisis on top of everything else. "Sorry. Go on, Clara."

"When he left, I went in and fished this out of the toilet. It's partially burnt, but looks like it might be in Japanese? I think?"

I took it carefully. The moment my fingers touched the wet, charred paper, a vision hit: Ben alone in a dimly lit room, carefully examining what appeared to be some kind of official document with Japanese characters. His hands shook as he read it, then folded it carefully and shoved it into his pocket. The vision was crystal clear: it had happened recently. Tonight. Because I recognized the wallpaper in the downstairs bathroom.

"What is this?" I whispered.

Jenny peered at the charred scrap. "Wait, I have an app that can translate this."

"Are you getting WiFi?" I asked.

She shook her head. "It's an offline app. You point your camera at it..." She pulled out her phone, and while she was tapping on her screen, my headlamp flickered once, twice, then died.

"Oh, come on," I muttered, tapping the light on my head. "These were supposed to be emergency lights."

"Maybe the battery died?" Clara suggested.

"They're USB powered," Jenny said, peering at my device, then twisting my lamp between her fingers. I leaned over to give her a better look. "Crap. There's no battery compartment."

"Of course there isn't." I yanked the now-useless device off my head. "Jimbo probably thought he was being eco-friendly."

"Maybe there are more headlamps?" Clara asked.

"Maybe. I'll check in a minute. Both of your lamps are working. Let's translate this paper with your app."

Jenny angled her phone camera at the burnt paper, squinting at the screen. "It's a receipt, I think. Look at these lines. Hang on, the app is processing."

I scrunched up my face. How was she getting the app to work without the internet? Was that possible? Apparently it was. I racked my brain, trying to remember what the guy at the phone store told me months ago. I was about to ask when Clara's headlamp began to flicker. She tapped it with growing panic. "No, no, not now."

"Mom," Jenny's voice was tight. "While we wait, there's something else. When I was in the dining room, I found Ben's phone on the table. He must have set it down. And..." She swallowed hard. "He had his camera open to photos of me. Like, a bunch of them, from when I was gathering flowers outside. I didn't even notice him taking pictures."

My stomach clenched. "Photos?"

"All from tonight. And they're not like normal photos you'd take of someone helping at an event. They're..." she shuddered. "Kind of stalker-ish. Close-ups of my face and parts of my body when I wasn't looking."

Clara's headlamp gave one final burst, then died completely. We huddled closer to Jenny's remaining light.

"What the eff,…duck," I whispered, a feeling of sheer rage going through me. "I'm going to—"

"Hold that thought, Mom. Here we go," Jenny said, staring at her phone. "This is a fugu certification from Japan. Or was, before Ben tried to burn it. But look at the date. The fish expired two months ago."

In the wan light of Jenny's lone headlamp, the three of us looked at the translation app, then at each other, horrified.

"So Nico was trying to poison us," I said. "Or at the very least, trying to cut corners and put us all in danger."

"And Ben…" Jenny's voice trailed off.

"Ben…" I echoed. Ben was cutting corners, trying to hide evidence that Nico had potentially tainted fish. Had he done something to Nico? It sure seemed like he wanted something with my daughter. My head was a swirl of fury and fear.

"Sure seems like Ben is our prime suspect," Clara muttered. "Oh. Did anyone find Adam?"

Before I could answer, I felt Jenny edging closer to me. Seeking connection. Probably afraid. I put my arm around her and gave her a firm squeeze. "I found him. He's in the clear."

I gave them a brief rundown of my conversation with Adam, and my visions. All the while, my mind was spinning.

Nico.

Ben.

My daughter, in danger.

I thought back to earlier in the evening, how Ben hovered nearby while Jenny arranged flowers, offering to help with the heavy vases. How he'd volunteered to carry wine glasses. How I spotted him lingering in the doorway, staring at her with a goofy grin. At the time, it had seemed like simple politeness and maybe a sweet instant crush.

Instead he was taking creepy photos while working for an equally skeevy chef who was going to serve us expired toxic fish.

Now everything felt sinister. My protective mom mode ratcheted up another notch.

"We need a new plan," I said.

Clara nodded.

"Hold up," Jenny whispered, flashing her phone. "Let me do a quick search on Ben. I have one bar on my cell now. I'm curious if anything's out there. I know Nico tagged Ben's in an Instagram post at one point and maybe we can get his last name from that... here we go."

Clara and I huddled closer, watching Jenny's fingers fly over her screen. The wan beam of her headlamp illuminated her determined expression. I chewed on my cheek while we waited.

"Oh no," Jenny breathed. "Mom, look."

She tilted her phone so Clara and I could see. A news article from two years ago: "Photography Assistant Arrested for Stalking in Manhattan." The photo showed a younger Ben being led away by police.

"That's all I can find," Jenny said. "The rest is behind a paywall and my credit card's in the other room."

My mouth hung open. *What were we going to do?*

"Try calling 911 again," Clara suggested. "Maybe the cell towers are back up."

I pulled out my phone, and this time, it actually rang. "It's going through," I whispered excitedly. Clara pressed her hands into a prayer gesture, and Jenny made a little clapping motion with her fingers.

My heart leaped as a dispatcher answered, but the moment I started explaining everything, the line went dead. The "no service" message mocked me from my screen.

I heaved a sigh and swore for the first time in ages. Didn't even bother apologizing for it, either.

Clara touched my arm. "Do you have a landline?"

"Oh my word." I pressed my hand to my forehead. "Yes. Yes, we do. How could I forget? We have that old fashioned answering machine so we must."

I led them to the antique desk. There was no phone on top of the desk, and I had to admit, most of the calls were usually routed to my cell — or Jimbo's. I stared at the guest sign-in book and the tourist brochures.

"Where is it?" I opened a drawer, then another.

"Mom, I think it's here."

I whirled around to see Jenny pointing at the wall behind the desk. All I could see was an enormous gilt-framed mirror, one of Aunt Shirley's finds. The ornate frame was carved with roses and thorns that seemed to shift in the shadows.

Half-hidden into the frame was a rotary phone mounted on the wall, nearly invisible because it was painted in swirling gold and black, blending perfectly with the gilt frame. It was as if Salvador Dali had designed the thing.

"Of course." I moved toward it, highly doubting whether this thing even worked. I'd seen it before, naturally, and thought it was part of a funky statement piece.

My fingers trembled as I lifted the receiver.

"There's a dial tone," I said incredulously. My finger instinctively went to the 9 and dialed, bringing back memories of middle school in the 1980s. I then dialed a 1, and a 1.

"It's ringing!"

Then the line went dead. I clicked the receiver on and off a few times with my hands, and tried dialing again. And again. But the calls didn't connect, and the dial tone had vanished.

"Not working. Why is it suddenly not working?" I was ready to slam the receiver down, like I used to in the early 90s.

Jenny's face went pale in the beam of her headlamp. "What do we do now?"

"What does the weather app say? Is the storm almost over?"

My daughter hunched over her phone. "It says there's one more rain band and then it looks clear. We might be able to make a run for it."

I glanced between my daughter and Clara, my mind racing. We could try to get everyone out of the inn. Load everyone up in the Crescent Moon van. Or tell people to leave in their cars. But what about Mitzi? And Ben? We could confront Ben directly, but that might make things worse. We could—

"Hey."

The soft voice came from behind us. All three of us whirled around to find Ben standing in the doorway to the hall, his face half in shadow. He appeared to be holding some sort of phone cord. A cell charger? Or a landline cable?

"I was wondering if I could talk to Jenny for a minute? In private?"

Over my dead body, I almost yelled.

Nineteen

In my forty-eight years, I'd faced down ghosts, murderers, stubborn chin hair, and my ex-husband's scuzzy attorney.

But nothing prepared me for the sight of Ben standing in that doorway, holding what was clearly our severed phone line. Next to me, Jenny's lone working headlamp cast ominous shadows on his face. She reached for my hand. On the other side of her, Clara gripped Jenny's arm.

We were linked. A team. A united front.

As much as I wanted to rant and scream, to throat punch Ben and shove him out of my home, I knew I had to remain calm.

Through the windows, I could see the storm was finally weakening, the rain no longer coming in sideways sheets. Maybe that meant the police were on their way, but we weren't out of danger yet.

I had to stall. At least until I could attract the attention of the others in the parlor. But how?

Lightning silently strobed through the windows, turning Ben's face ominous and skeletal for a split second. It felt like we were suddenly in a horror movie, and I didn't appreciate that one bit. I've never liked scary movies.

"Jenny?" Ben's voice was soft, pleading. "Can we talk? Alone?"

"Absolutely not. You're getting nowhere near my daughter," I said in my most brittle, angriest, middle-aged-woman voice. It was so forceful that I felt Jenny flinch (probably because she'd only heard that tone coming from me once before, directed at her father.)

Ben's face changed then, hardened into something that made my gut clench. The meek assistant had disappeared, replaced by something darker. He stepped forward, the phone cord dangling from his hand like a threat.

He didn't like being challenged.

"You don't understand," he said, his voice low and menacing. "None of you understand. I did it for her. To protect her from him." His free hand gestured toward my apartment, where Nico's body lay. "He was going to do something to all of you, and hurt her too. Like he hurts everyone."

"Ben," Clara said softly, "put down the cord."

"I saw how he looked at her," Ben continued as if Clara hadn't spoken. "At Jenny. The way he looks at all pretty girls. And then he was going to serve that bad fish, probably make everyone sick for his stupid TikTok views. He had a plan to make a few of you sick, then step in as a hero somehow. I couldn't let that happen."

He was raving mad, making no sense. I felt Jenny trembling behind me, but her voice was steady. "You took pictures of me. You did that, not Nico."

"Because you're different!" Ben took another step forward. The three of us inched back. "You're kind. And real. Not like his social media followers. I watched you help your mom, arrange flowers, make everyone feel welcome. I thought.... I thought if I could stop him, or even slow him down, I could show you what he was really like. And plus... I just wanted a photo or two of you. I was going to show you."

Thunder rumbled in the distance, softer now. Retreating. Jenny shivered.

My mind reeled. In the parlor, I could hear one of the last songs in the movie. I needed to try to get the others' attention because we were alone with a madman. But, the three of us could take him, right?

Maybe? If he didn't have a weapon. He was only holding the cord, but who knew what was in the pocket of his jeans? My brain was going in every direction.

"Ben," I said carefully, "why don't we all sit down and talk about this? I can make some tea."

"Talk?" He laughed, a hollow sound that made my skin crawl. "That's all anyone ever does. Talk. Write reports. File complaints. Nobody ever actually stops people like Nico."

"What do you mean, people like Nico?" Clara asked. Her voice was gentle, like she was soothing a spooked horse.

With one hand, he wound the phone cord around the fingers of his other hand. "You don't know what he was really like. The stealing, that was only the beginning. He'd take things from clients' homes during private chef gigs. Personal things. Important things." His eyes darted toward my apartment., where Nico's body was stretched out on my kitchen floor. "Like the stuff in his bag upstairs."

My heart stuttered. He knew about the bag. Did he go upstairs and discover the bag had been searched, its stolen contents gone?

What about Mitzi?

"But it wasn't just theft," Ben continued, his voice taking on a ranting monotone. "He'd humiliate people. His assistants, his clients. Anyone he thought was beneath him. He'd film them without permission, edit the videos to make them look stupid. There are dozens of clips he never posted. He kept them to prove he had power over people."

"Did you poison him?" Jenny asked quietly.

Ben's face crumpled. "I only wanted him to pass out! To ruin his big night, maybe get him to stop being so horrible to everyone. I crushed up some of my prescription sleeping pills and slipped them into that stupid blue cocktail while I was filming. He was so focused on looking sexy for the camera, he never even noticed."

He began to tremble, hard. Clearly he was coming unglued. "And that wasn't even the worst part. He made me steal things for him. I mean, he stole things too. We both did. The crystals from Clara's purse, Mitzi's pen... he'd point to what he wanted and I had to get them while he distracted everyone with his performances. Said if I didn't, he'd ruin my career. Just like he ruined everything else." His voice cracked. "I didn't mean to... I didn't know he'd... what have I done?"

Suddenly, his expression shifted from anguish to desperate determination. Before I could react, he lunged forward and tried to grab Jenny's arm. We held around her wrists and hands. Ben tugged in one direction, Clara and I in the other.

Jenny's headlamp took this moment to flicker for a few beats. In that moment in the darkness, Ben moved with unexpected, frightening, speed. He shoved Clara hard enough to make her stumble backward into me. As we both lost our balance, his hand shot out and grabbed Jenny, yanking her roughly from my grasp.

I grunted, and Clara yelped.

Jenny's headlamp returned, shining brighter than ever.

"Stay back and don't say a word!" He hissed. "I can't go to jail. I can't. Jenny understands. Don't you, Jenny? You saw how awful he was. We have a connection, right?"

My heart nearly stopped as I watched my daughter in the grip of an increasingly unstable man. Jenny stood still, but I could see her trembling.

"Ben, honey," I said, fighting to keep my voice calm while every maternal instinct screamed at me to attack. "You're scaring her. This isn't you. You're not like Nico. You don't hurt people. Least of all Jenny."

His hands shook. "I already killed someone. What difference does it make now?"

"It makes all the difference," Clara said softly. "You didn't mean to kill him. But what you're doing right now? This is a choice."

I watched my daughter's face, seeing both fear and something else. It was a flicker of that same fierceness I'd noticed earlier when she told me about Sedona. About the lights in the sky. My brave, complicated girl who'd faced her own terrors and now a terrible man.

"Ben," Jenny said, her voice shaking but clear. "My mom's right. This isn't you. Let's talk, okay? I want to listen."

"I'm worried you'll hate me," he whispered, but his grip on her arm loosened slightly. "You don't know me."

"No," Jenny said, a touch too quickly.

My throat felt tight, watching them. Maybe he was a lost, lonely young man who'd made a terrible mistake. Maybe he was a psychopath. It didn't matter, and I wasn't going to make excuses for him.

He had my daughter, my baby, and that changed everything. I thought of all the times I'd protected Jenny, from bullies in elementary school, from her nightmares in middle school, from her own self-doubts. But I couldn't protect her from this by force.

"Actually, I think we do know you," I said quietly. "You're someone who wanted to stop a bully. Who couldn't stand watching Nico hurt people anymore. That's not the same as being a killer. You wanted to make things right."

Clara nodded vigorously. "Absolutely."

Please let this work, I thought. The air was heavy with more tension than I'd ever felt in my life. Oddly, a scent hit my nostrils: that same lavender scent from earlier. My senses must be going haywire with all the adrenaline coursing through my body. I felt like I was practically vibrating.

Ben's breathing was ragged. The phone cord slipped from his fingers, landing on the floor with a soft thud. I longed to lunge for it, to remove at least that threat from the situation.

"Let's go sit in the library where it's more comfortable, and have some water. I'm thirsty," Jenny said. "Please?"

Ben nodded slowly, still holding Jenny's arm but no longer gripping it so tightly. They took a few steps toward the library doorway, Jenny carefully matching his pace.

I followed close enough to grab her if needed, my fingers curled into fists at my sides. Clara moved with me, bending to scoop up the discarded phone cord in one fluid motion.

I flashed her a quick thumbs up while wondering if anyone in the parlor could hear us. They were talking about the movie, and I pondered whether to scream and alert everyone.

No, that wouldn't be a good idea right at this second. Not until I figured out whether Ben had a weapon on him.

The library felt different in the dim light of Jenny's headlamp. Shadows danced on the bookshelves, and rain tapped against the windows, softer now. Ben sank onto the sofa, tugging Jenny next to him.

Clara settled into a chair near the door, the cord now hidden in the folds of her jersey dress. I remained standing.

"You're making me nervous," Ben said. "Sit. Uh, please."

I nodded and took a seat in a hard wooden chair near the shelf containing my aunt's spell books. My gaze darted around the room, from the door to Jenny, to Clara, back to Jenny, and then to the entrance to my apartment.

The bookcase door was still closed. I cleared my throat.

"Tell us about working with Nico," I said quietly.

Ben's shoulders slumped. "At first, it was amazing. I thought I'd learn so much. But he..." He swallowed hard. "He'd make me reshoot the same scene fifty times. Call me stupid. Fat. Ugly. He knew I couldn't quit because I needed the exposure, the connections."

"That must have been awful," Clara murmured. "Being taken advantage of."

"I lost twenty pounds. Imagine that. Working for a chef and losing weight. Started having panic attacks. And then the stealing started." Ben pressed his palms into his eyes. "He made me help him take things. Said if I didn't, he'd ruin my career."

"Is that why you took the pictures of Jenny?" I asked. "Because Nico made you—"

Ben's head snapped up. "No! Those were mine. I took them because..." His hand went to his pocket, then his eyes went wide with panic. He patted his jeans frantically. "Where is it? What did you do with the cord?"

Twenty

"Let's not worry about the cord now. You're not going to need it. It's safe," I said quietly, watching Ben's fingers tremble as they patted his empty pockets. He had to have cut it with something, and I didn't want to find out what. "Just like Jenny is safe. Just like you're safe right now, even though it doesn't feel that way."

His head snapped up, eyes wild. "Safe? I killed someone tonight!"

"By accident," I reminded him. "Because you were trying to stop someone who hurt people." I shifted slightly in the wooden chair. "I understand feeling powerless. When I got divorced, when I moved here... there were so many times I felt like I had no control."

"We've all felt powerless before, Ben," Clara said softly. Jenny nodded. I did, too.

Ben's breathing was ragged, but he was listening. Jenny remained still beside him on the sofa.

"Tell me about the stealing," I said softly. "About why Nico took those things."

"He couldn't help himself." Ben's voice cracked. "It wasn't about value or meaning. He'd take anything. Paperclips from office desks. Sugar packets from cafes. A child's hair ribbon at a catering job. He'd collect things. Keep them organized in little bags and boxes at his warehouse."

"Kleptomania," Clara murmured. "So those things had no magical significance?"

Ben shook his head. "It was just stuff that meant something to him. He'd steal, and tell me what to take."

"Ben, what happened tonight was tragic," I said. "But we can help you through this. You're not alone. Together we can work it out."

"You think?" His voice quavered.

"Absolutely," Clara said firmly. "I'll bet the police will understand. I was married to a cop. I know."

"Really?" Ben sniffled.

Men and their need for constant reassurance, I thought sourly. Still, if it kept my daughter safe, I'd promise him the moon.

"Absolutely." I nodded vigorously.

"I'm so sorry you had to deal with his abuse," Clara added. Her voice held a warm, caring tone.

"Hurt people hurt people," Jenny said. "That's what I learned in my psychology class."

"You get it," Ben said, turning to her and taking her hand. "I knew you would."

Jenny finally turned towards Ben. Really looked at him, as if for the first time. "I do have a question, though."

"Tell me," he replied.

"Why did Nico have a notebook with all the guests' names? And the comments, like 'useful.' What was that about?"

Ben winced. "You saw that?"

"Yeah, we went through the bag," I chimed in, then a terrible thought hit me. "It was his, wasn't it? Not yours?"

That lavender scent that had been teasing me all evening suddenly intensified. Maybe it was Clara? And yet, I hadn't smelled it on her upstairs. I took a giant, fortifying inhale. It felt like the first breath I'd taken in hours.

Ben rolled his eyes. "Yeah, it was his notebook. He liked to write down observations about everyone at his parties. To jog his memory. It was stupid. Everything he did was absurd. I can't believe I ever got involved with him."

"I see," Jenny said, nodding slowly as if she was working up to ask another question.

"I knew you were kind from the moment I met you," Ben said, his grip on Jenny's arm loosening slightly. "That's why I stayed. I could have left during the storm, but I wanted you to know the truth about him. About everything." His voice took on an uncomfortably intimate tone. "You're different from the others. You see things clearly."

"The only thing I see clearly is that you're delusional," Jenny said.

At first, I was about to panic that my daughter was talking back to a madman. But something flickered in the corner of my vision. At first I thought it was Jenny's headlamp acting up again, but no. This was different. A faint, golden shimmer near the desk where I'd attempted my protection spell earlier. Somehow I hadn't managed to sweep in that area, and a small clump of herbs I'd scattered were still there, hidden under the edge of the desk where I'd kicked them. I think they were mixed with something. I could barely see.

Was that a tumbleweed of cat fur?

Was my lackluster housekeeping ability paying off? Or was that some Freddie magic? Or...

Ben must have spotted something in my expression. He held Jenny's hand in both of his. "What are you looking at, Amelia?"

"Nothing," I said quickly. Too quickly.

"You're lying." His voice rose. "Everyone lies. Nico lied. The producers lied. The restaurant critics lied—"

"Ben," Jenny interrupted softly. "You're hurting my hand."

The golden shimmer pulsed stronger, and the lavender scent was back. It was incredibly strong now, almost pungent. Was it from the herbs I'd used earlier? Or maybe from Jenny's shampoo?

Either way, something was building in the room. Something protective. I could feel it.

Something maternal and feminine and *strong*.

Ben's eyes darted around. "What's that smell? What are you doing?"

"I smell it too," Clara said softly. "It reminds me of my grandmother's garden. She always said lavender was strongest when women stood together."

"Stay cool." I said, but this time my voice was steady. Calm. I could feel the energy gathering, like static electricity before a storm. "Ben, let go of my daughter. Now."

"Or what?" He tried to sound threatening, but his voice cracked. "You'll call the police? They're not coming. No one's coming."

That's when I noticed Clara's gaze. She was trying not to look at something to my right, but I could tell she was having a difficult time tearing her eyes away. I subtly shifted and what I saw nearly made me gasp.

A bright glow was shining from the top of the little plain black wastebasket near the desk. Not like fire, but more like a steady, golden light.

What was going on? It had to be the protection herbs, the lavender mix that I'd unceremoniously swept into the bin. It was the only possible answer. *But how?* Hadn't the spell failed because I was interrupted by Nico?

I glanced over at Jenny. Her expression was one of pure, rapt attention at the spectacle unfolding in the garbage can. The golden light bathed her pretty face, making her look angelic. *My baby.* Her headlamp pulsed three times, then flickered out.

The light in the room, however, grew stronger. It was like sunrise, golden and hopeful. It seemed — no, it felt — like it was drawing strength from all three of us. My maternal protection, Clara's steadfast support, and Jenny's own inner power, all combining with the herbs I'd scattered earlier.

Maybe magic needed the right moment to prove its strength.

"Mom, look," she whispered.

The shimmer flowed over the rim of the wastebasket and spread across the wood floor, over the Persian rug, like a river of honey. It crept toward the center of the room.

As it reached Clara, she gasped softly. The phone cord in her lap began to glow and uncoil like a living thing.

"Oh!" she breathed. In a serpentine motion, the cord freed itself from her pocket and into the shifting light.

Ben's grip on Jenny's wrist tightened. "What's happening? What are you women doing? Oh my God, you're really witches, aren't you? That wasn't a joke!"

"I'm not doing anything," I said truthfully. Well, not anymore. Whatever was happening now seemed to have a mind of its own. The protection spell I'd botched earlier had apparently needed time to work its magic. Like bread dough rising or cookies cooling. Some things couldn't be rushed.

Then I smiled. "But yes. I'm really a witch."

The glowing cord rose from the floor, now impossibly long, as if it had borrowed length from every phone line in town. It twisted through the golden light like a snake charmed by music only it could hear.

"Ben," Jenny said softly, "it's okay. Let go."

He shook his head frantically, but I could see the fight leaving him. The magical light lapped at his feet like gentle waves, and the cord began to wind itself around his ankles. Not cruelly, but firmly. The light writhed its way up Ben's legs, toward his torso.

"I don't understand," he whispered, his grip on Jenny finally loosening. "What is this?"

"It's protection," I said, watching as the cord continued its work, securing his wrists with the same gentle but unshakeable force. "From a mother who's had more than enough excitement for one evening."

The cord wound its way around Ben's arms and torso several times, immobilizing him. He tried to struggle, but he was no match for the persistent encircling.

Jenny slipped free and hurried to me. I stood and wrapped my arms around her, breathing in the familiar scent of her shampoo mixed with the lavender from my spell. The golden light swirled around us both like a warm embrace.

"It's okay. It's all okay." Tears filled my eyes.

Ben sat on the sofa, now thoroughly bound, but looking more bewildered than afraid. The anger had drained from his face, replaced by something that looked almost like relief.

Clara stood and smoothed her dress. "Well," she said with remarkably steady composure for someone who'd witnessed a magical phone cord protection spell. "Wow. I sure didn't expect that."

I extended an arm, indicating Clara should join us for the group hug. She did, and the golden light filled the room, warm and comforting, yet incredibly vibrant. Somehow I knew it would hold until help arrived. My botched protection spell might have taken its sweet time to work, but like many things in life — from new beginnings to motherhood to magic — sometimes the best results came from letting things unfold in their own time.

The three of us stood wrapped in our group hug while the gold shimmer continued to pulse gently around us. Jenny's tears dampened my shoulder, but I could feel her smiling. Perhaps it wasn't merely the magic making the room feel warmer. Maybe it was the collective power of the three of us, connected in this strange moment.

Footsteps approached from the hallway. "Hey, Amelia, do you have any snacks? Sarah's getting hangry and the movie's almost... whoa, what's going on here?"

The three of us broke apart. Marc stood in the doorway. He had a green knitted afghan draped over his tall frame. His eyes darted from the glowing room to Ben (still thoroughly immobilized in the magically-elongated phone cord) to our tearful group hug.

"We're having a moment," I said.

He blinked several times. "I mean, the floating golden light is new, but honestly? After tonight, I'd believe anything. Why is Ben tied up like that? Oh. Oh! It must have something to do with Nico. Is this like a citizen's arrest or something?"

"Sort of," Clara said, wiping her eyes. I couldn't tell if she was crying or laughing.

"Yeah," I said.

Marc chewed on the inside of his cheek for a second. "Do you need my help? Want me to get the others?"

I shook my head and waved him off.

Clara looked to Ben, who was oddly calm in the bright gold light. "Nah," she said. "We're good."

In the distance, a siren wailed. It sounded like it was coming closer.

"The bad news is, I don't think snacks are on the menu for the rest of the night," I aOded, thinking grimly of what was in the kitchen. "Maybe check the dining room? Mitzi raided my cheese drawer earlier and I think I saw an unopened box of Triscuits. I'd grab those while you can."

Marc nodded. "Right. Got it. I'll just... go do that then. Carry on."

He backed out slowly while shaking his head. "This place is *wild*," he muttered as he retreated.

Jenny laughed softly against my shoulder, and I hugged her tighter. I never wanted to let go.

The golden glow faded slowly, like sunset in reverse, and at that exact moment, every light in the inn blazed to life. The sudden brightness made us all blink, and even Ben whispered, "Finally."

The three of us looked at him, then at each other. We were all incredulous.

Even the old-fashioned sconces in the library, the ones that hadn't worked since I inherited the place, were now casting a warm glow. Hunh. Suppose I should consult an electrician about that.

Through the windows, I could see the town's streetlights winking on one by one, as if by magic. Or perhaps Florida Power and Light had fixed the electric grid. Either way, the timing felt significant and serendipitous.

I half expected Ben to struggle now that the magic had left the building, but he didn't. Instead, he remained securely bound by the mysteriously elongated phone cord, which had somehow retained a faint luminescence. The whole thing reminded me of how Christmas lights would continue to sparkle for a few seconds after being unplugged.

"You saw what?" Sarah Anderson's voice drifted in from the hallway. "Marc, honey, are you sure? Are you exaggerating again?"

"I know what I saw," Marc insisted. "It was like... like the whole room was full of light. As if someone had poured liquid gold everywhere."

"No way," Kristan pointed out. "Maybe it was lightning?"

"Through the walls?" Marc sounded exasperated. "Listen, I know it sounds crazy, but—"

They appeared in the doorway, a cluster of confused faces. Their expressions shifted from skepticism to shock as they took in the scene: Ben trussed up like a holiday turkey, Clara and Jenny flanking me protectively, and the scent of lavender in the air.

Adam pushed through the group. "What in the world?" His gaze landed on Ben, then on me. "Did you...? Did he...?" He gestured vaguely at the bindings.

"He confessed," I said simply. The less said about magical phone cords, the better. "To killing Nico."

A collective gasp went up from the group. Sarah pressed closer to Marc, who wrapped an arm around her shoulders.

"But how did you tie him up?" Kristan asked, her professional demeanor cracking slightly. She looked from Ben to me and back again. "And what's that smell? It's like a spa in here."

"Maybe it was a protection spell," Marc blurted. "Remember, we learned about that in the spellcasting workshop. There was this light, and the cord just—" He broke off as Sarah elbowed him while rolling her eyes. "What? It's true!"

The corners of my mouth tugged up. I caught Clara's eye and she waggled her brows, which made Jenny snort.

The sirens grew louder. Multiple vehicles, from the sound of it. Red and blue lights began to strobe through the windows.

"Looks like the cops are finally here. I'll get the door, so the three of you can keep an eye on Ben," Adam offered, already moving toward the foyer.

"Thanks," I called out.

Ben sat perfectly still, his face a mask of resignation. The fight had completely drained out of him, replaced by something that looked almost like peace. Maybe coming clean had been a relief. Or perhaps the spell had sedated him.

"Someone should check on Mitzi," Clara said softly.

"I will," Jenny volunteered, probably glad for something practical to do. "Is that okay, Mom?"

"Sure is. You two are old pals at this point."

She slipped out of the room and up the stairs as I heard Adam open the door. Footsteps approached. Two paramedics appeared first, laden with equipment and looking soggy. They must have waded through some serious flooding to reach us.

"Sorry we're so late. It's been a helluva night. We got a report of a possible poisoning?" the first one asked, glancing around the crowded room. "Who's the patient?"

"Through there." I pointed through the hidden bookcase door toward my apartment. "But I'm afraid you're too late."

"Uh, what about this guy?" The second paramedic gestured to Ben.

"He's fine. We need to wait for the police on him," Clara said.

I led the paramedics toward my kitchen, where Nico still lay under the crocheted afghan. I forced myself not to look at his shoes sticking out from under the cover.

More sirens approached, and soon the inn was swarming with police officers. They weren't the faces I was used to dealing with, and frankly, I kind of missed Chief Wolf's stern yet commanding presence. (I also couldn't wait to hear what he had to say about all this, because surely someone would contact him while he was on his Alaskan cruise with Liz).

The officers were kind and moved with practiced efficiency, securing the scene and separating everyone for statements. Although they seemed a bit haggard from the storm, they didn't seem phased by our citizen's arrest or the fact that our suspect was tied up with an extra-long phone cord.

Then again, I supposed they'd seen a lot weirder in Cypress Grove.

A detective named Marina Martinez took charge, her dark

hair pulled back in a severe bun. She didn't bat an eye at the hidden bookcase entrance or the gothic décor, which made me wonder if she was a Cypress Grove native.

"Ms. Matthews?" She approached me with a tablet in hand. "I understand this is your inn?"

I nodded, suddenly exhausted. The adrenaline that had carried me through the evening was wearing off, leaving me shaky and unsettled.

"Can you tell me what happened tonight?" she said.

"Sure. But would you mind if we talked in private, and if I had a small, yet fortifying, glass of whiskey while we chat?"

She glanced at Ben, then at my gaggle of guests, who were clustered together on one side of the room.

"Fine by me. Wish I could have one," she declared. "Gosh, it smells good in here. Like a spa. You're going to have to tell me what kind of candles you use. Is that lavender?"

Detective Martinez commandeered half my dining room table, with a bit of help from Kristan, who had cleared away the wine glasses and empty cracker boxes.

The wine stains on the tablecloth were covered with coffee cups from Joe's Java Junction — an officer had brought in a few boxes of the stuff, because apparently that was the only place open during the storm. The scent of dark roast competed with the lingering lavender.

Clara sat across from Martinez, speaking in a low voice while a young officer took notes. I heard fragments about true crime podcasts and Victorian poison gardens. Clara's hands moved expressively as she talked, and for the first time since she'd arrived, she looked animated rather than exhausted.

Thankfully, Martinez seemed to be taking her seriously, nodding at Clara's words.

I was about to grab another cup of coffee when I heard insistent footsteps. I assumed they were from another cop — they kept coming in — but then Oliver burst in, the lenses of his black-rimmed glasses slightly rain-flecked and his usual professorial composure replaced by sheer worry. His beard was a bit scruffier than usual, and his T-shirt looked extra wrinkled.

"Amelia! Honey!" He crossed the room in three long strides. "Are you okay? I tried calling but couldn't get through. The radio said there was a death at the inn, and then the storm—"

I practically melted into his arms, not caring that the room was full of police officers and guests. His familiar scent of books and coffee wrapped around me like a warm blanket.

"I'm fine," I murmured against his chest. "It's been quite a night."

A young man about Jenny's age appeared in the doorway behind Oliver. He was tall, with warm brown skin and a brilliant smile that somehow managed to light up the already well-lit room. His curly hair was slightly damp from the rain, and he wore a WBOO t-shirt under a leather jacket.

"Hey, Ms. Matthews," he said, his voice carrying the smooth cadence of someone used to being on air. "Sorry to crash your crime scene. Oliver and I were jamming and he's been worried, so I offered to drive him here in my Jeep."

"Calvin," I smiled at him. "And it's Amelia, remember?"

The detective looked over. "Friends of yours?" she asked, though her tone suggested she already knew the answer.

"Oliver Everhart," Oliver supplied, leaning over with his hand extended. "I'm a professor at—"

"The paranormal researcher," Martinez interrupted. "I've read your work on the haunted springs. And you," she nodded at Calvin, "are DJ Ghostwave. My kid loves your late-night show."

Calvin's grin widened. "Always nice to meet a fan's mom."

"Yeah, she's really into your 'high vibes' show on Sunday night," Martinez added.

While Calvin chatted with Martinez about his late-night radio show, Oliver pulled me aside. "What happened here? Why are the cops here—"

The click of sensible shoes in the hallway interrupted us, and we looked over. A tall woman about my age, wearing navy scrubs appeared. Dr. Heather Yates carried her medical examiner's kit and wore an expression that suggested she'd seen it all before.

Jenny chose that exact moment to return from checking on Mitzi. She remained in the doorway, her eyes meeting Calvin's. Her gaze then fell on Oliver, then back to Calvin.

"Jenny?" I said.

"Oliver?" Jenny replied.

Calvin stared at Jenny, a goofy grin on his face. "Heyyyy," he said to Jenny softly.

"Calvin?" Heather raised an eyebrow at her son.

"Dr. Yates," I nodded.

Startled from basking in my daughter's beauty — young people! Didn't they know this was a crime scene? — Calvin then looked guiltily between his mother and me. "Mom?"

Detective Martinez shook her head and turned back to Clara.

We all stood there for a moment, looking at each other in a circle of confusion and recognition. Even Clara glanced over from her interview, trying to follow who knew whom.

"Sorry," she waved at us then focused on the detective.

Heather Yates broke the silence with a laugh. "Well, this is delightfully awkward. But there's a body in the kitchen that needs my attention, so the introductions will have to wait." She patted Calvin's cheek as she passed. "Though I expect a full explanation of why you're at a crime scene instead of the radio station, young man."

"Mom?" Calvin's eyebrows shot up. "I thought you were off tonight?"

"I was," she said dryly. "Until the state attorney's office called." She turned to me. "Amelia, what kind of trouble have you gotten into now?"

"Well, uh, this was supposed to be a pop-up dinner party," I said.

Jenny sidled up to me, her eyes now on Oliver. She extended her hand. "Hi," she said, almost shyly. "I didn't get a chance to properly introduce myself at the festival last night. I'm Jenny, Amelia's daughter."

I winced. "That was only last night?"

"Jenny, it's a pleasure to finally meet you." Oliver gave a formal little bow, then shook my daughter's hand.

Calvin leaned into our group and said in a low voice, "What's this about a body?"

"It's a long story," I said, right as Heather called out from my apartment.

"Amelia? A word?"

I glanced at Jenny.

"I'll fill them in," she said, her cheeks tinged with red.

I hesitated, wondering why she seemed so eager to recount the traumatic evening. Probably shock. I nodded and squeezed her arm before I left.

In my apartment, Heather knelt beside Nico's body. She'd pulled back the afghan and was peering at his face, gently touching his cheeks with blue-gloved hands.

"Didn't I talk with you a couple of weeks ago regarding another dead guy?" she asked without looking up. "Though I have to say, this is an interesting one. Have you moved anything or shifted the body in any way?"

"Just covered him with the afghan," I said. "The blue liquid on the floor is from his cocktail. He was drinking it right before he collapsed. He was a chef. Doing a pop-up event. Apparently famous from TikTok."

Heather sat back and nodded slowly. "The state attorney mentioned something about sleeping pills in a confession?"

"His assistant Ben told us he crushed some up and put them in Nico's drink."

She pursed her lips, then picked up Nico's stiff arm and

inspected his skin, running her fingers over his knuckles. She pinched the back of his hand. "Is the perp still here?"

"No, officers took him down to the station about a half hour ago."

"Hmph. A TikTok chef." She set Nico's hand down and gazed at him from head to toe, then squinted up at me. "Why's he shirtless?"

I shook my head and sighed. "I'm still not really sure."

Twenty-Two

"She's fine," Jenny reported, returning downstairs from checking on Mitzi for the third time. "She woke up briefly and wanted to know how she got upstairs. I told her we helped her, then put a glass of water and some Advil on the nightstand. She's back asleep now."

I smiled at my daughter's thoughtfulness. Her hair was a total mess, yet it still somehow looked fashionable. It was difficult to believe that a little over twenty-four hours ago, she'd arrived at the summer solstice festival and was scandalized by my witchy ways. Now here she was, caring for a drunk city council member after helping take down a murderer with my magic.

"Thanks, honey." I reached to squeeze her arm.

The activity around us was still chaotic, and had been for hours. The guests had cycled through the dining room to make their statements to detectives, and teams of crime scene investigators, medical examiner staff, and state attorneys wandered in and out.

I had my hands full directing everyone this way and that (while also keeping the coffee flowing), while Oliver took it upon himself to make sure Freddie didn't escape. He also chatted with the various law enforcement folks he knew from around town, probably trying to glean more details about the night, since I'd been warned not to discuss the case just yet.

Adam had finished his statement and was gathering his things, looking drained but relieved. Sarah and Marc Anderson huddled together near the stairs, clearly ready to retreat to their room. The crime scene techs moved efficiently through my apartment, their equipment cases and evidence bags creating an odd rhythm of clicks and rustles.

Kristan approached, her tablet clutched to her chest like a shield. "I should head out. The flooding's receded enough that I can make it home." She paused, then added softly, "I'm so sorry about all this, Amelia. This isn't how I wanted the Chamber's first pop-up dinner to go."

"Not your fault," I assured her. "You didn't know Nico was going to show up shirtless, try to poison us with expired fugu, and steal a bunch of our stuff."

She let out a soft groan of dissatisfaction. "God, no. I knew he was a bit of a character from his social media, but this…" She blew out a breath. "I'll call you tomorrow about damage control. I'll be sending out a news release and doing a press conference at the chamber office. You don't have to attend. I'll take the fall for this."

"I appreciate that about the press conference, but really. Don't blame yourself. You did the best you could. I'm happy to write a letter to whoever, telling them you still have my full confidence as a business owner in town."

"Thanks." Her bottom lip trembled, and I wondered if her careful façade was about to crack.

As she collected her things, Clara appeared at my elbow, looking as exhausted as I felt.

"I think I'll head up to my room," she said. "Though I'm not sure I'll sleep much tonight."

"Thank you," I said softly. "For everything."

She smiled. "That's what friends are for, right? Even brand new ones who show up uninvited during a murder investigation."

"I'll walk you out," Clara said to Kristan, who looked more

shaken than at any time during the previous hours. The two friends moved toward the foyer, and I heard Kristan's voice crack. "I can't believe I brought him here. Can't believe I brought you into this, when you're going through so much personally. Into this town."

"Stop," Clara said firmly. "You couldn't have known."

Their voices faded as they stepped outside. A few minutes later, Clara returned alone, her face drawn with concern. "Kristan's pretty shaken up. I made her promise to text when she gets home." She took a deep inhale. "I'm toast."

"We all are." I touched her arm. "Thank you for everything tonight."

She managed a tired smile and gave me a weary half-hug. Unlike when we were hugging as a group in the library, all of Clara's energy was gone. Mine was too, most likely.

"What a way to start my new life in Florida, right?" she said as she climbed the stairs.

"It's all uphill from here," I said. "Or is it downhill?"

We laughed and waved goodnight.

"Mrs. Matthews?" Sarah Anderson's voice was barely above a whisper. She and Marc stood awkwardly nearby. "We're headed upstairs."

"Good idea. Get some rest," I told them. "And Sarah? It's Amelia."

Marc nodded. "Thanks for, well, everything. The magic and all that. It was pretty amazing. One of the best parts of our honeymoon."

Sarah giggled. "Babe, I think you were seeing things. Lightning can play tricks on your eyes."

As they headed upstairs, still debating what Marc had witnessed in the library, Adam approached. He'd pulled himself together.

"I've given my statement to the cops and should get home, unless you need anything," he said.

I shook my head and told him to head out.

"Jason's probably worried sick. The puppy too." He paused. "Listen, Amelia. I'm sorry about tonight. If I'd known Nico would be here... maybe without my presence, he wouldn't have acted the way he did."

"Highly doubtful," I said firmly. "And you helped us understand what kind of person he really was. Go home to Jason and your fur baby."

He smiled tiredly, then turned to Jenny, who was mid-yawn. "Thanks. Jenny, it was nice to meet you, despite the circumstances. Stop by Grape Escape sometime. Your mom's a regular."

Jenny nodded. "Sorry for yawning. We're all exhausted. And I will. Thanks."

"She turned twenty-one recently so I guess she can have a half glass of wine," I joked.

"Mom."

Adam and I looked at each other and shook our heads, then hugged. "See you soon," I whispered.

I was about to suggest that Jenny also go upstairs, to one of the empty guest rooms. There was no way either one of us could sleep in my apartment tonight, since the crime scene techs would likely be here for hours. It was three in the morning, and they hadn't even started processing the scene for fingerprints. I'd meant to find out how long it would take, since I had a new crop of guests coming tomorrow (or was it today, I was so tired I'd lost track of time). If the techs and police were going to be here for days, I needed to give everyone a heads up — and refunds.

In my nine months at the inn, I'd never had to give a refund. There was a first for everything, I guessed.

Detective Martinez emerged from my apartment, followed by Oliver and Calvin. Dr. Yates trailed behind them, pulling off her latex gloves with an efficient snap.

"Not a chance, you two," she said, though her stern tone held a hint of amusement. "I can't release anything until the official autopsy is finished. I should have a preliminary report later today or tomorrow. And I mean it. This is an active investigation."

"Come on, Dr. Y," Calvin said. "Give a hint? For your favorite late-night DJ?"

"That's Dr. Mom to you, and no. Not even for my favorite DJ son." She dropped the gloves in a medical waste bag. "Though I have to say, Oliver, this is different from our coffee meetups last year. Remember how we spent an hour debating the historical accuracy of those ghost stories at Shell Manor?"

"Mom," Calvin groaned. "We agreed never to mention your brief romance with my bro. It's weird enough that you both show up at my paranormal roundtable discussions."

"It was two coffee dates," Oliver said, adjusting his glasses. "Hardly a romance."

"And now look at us," Dr. Yates said, smiling at me and Jenny. "All tied up in another Cypress Grove mystery, but with Amelia and her daughter. Imagine that."

"Speaking of mysteries," Calvin turned to Jenny, "you should totally call in to my show sometime. We do this thing at around two in the morning where people share their weird experiences. Ghost stories, UFO sightings, whatever." He shrugged. "If you're into that kind of thing."

Jenny's tired eyes sparked with interest. "Really?"

"The body's been transported, Detective," Dr. Yates called to Martinez. "I'll start the preliminary examination in a few hours." She checked her watch. "Oof. I'm going to need a vat of coffee for this."

"Mom, need a ride? My Jeep handled the flooding like a champ." Calvin looked at her with concern.

"No, I've got the county van." She turned to me. "Amelia, try to get some rest. I suspect we'll be talking again soon."

A young man in scrubs emerged from my apartment. "Dr. Yates? Everything's loaded and ready."

"Thanks, Stevie." She gathered her kit. "I'll see you all soon. Too soon, probably, knowing this town." She gave us a tired wave and followed her assistant out.

"So these UFO calls," Jenny was saying to Calvin, "do people ever mention seeing patterns? Like, in the lights?"

My head snapped around, though I tried to appear casual about it. My mom radar was definitely activated.

"Oh yeah," Calvin said enthusiastically. "Especially over the Gulf. We get all kinds of reports about geometric shapes, usually around two AM. That's why I call it the witching hour segment."

"Really?" Jenny sounded interested, but I couldn't be sure. Was it relief? Recognition?

Oliver was saying something about bringing breakfast for the guests in the morning, but I couldn't focus. I was too busy straining to hear Jenny ask Calvin why he wasn't broadcasting tonight.

"When the weather's gnarly, the station meteorologist takes over..." Calvin launched into a discussion about his hours at the station, and I wondered if he was trying to impress my daughter.

"Amelia?" Oliver touched my shoulder. "Did you hear what I said about the coffee cake?"

"Hmm? Oh, sorry." I turned back to him, my mind spinning. "Um, that sounds good, I guess. Or a dozen donuts will be fine."

Detective Martinez drifted back toward my apartment, speaking in low tones with one of the techs who'd beckoned her over.

"Prof, we should probably head out," Calvin said, jingling his car keys. "I've got summer school class tomorrow." He turned to Jenny. "You should definitely call in sometime. Thursday nights are best. That's when all the weird stuff happens. I mean, you saw some weird tonight, I heard."

Jenny laughed, a genuine, bubbly sound. Her cheeks took on a rosy glow. "Yeah, we did."

"So what actually happened?" Calvin leaned forward, lowering his voice conspiratorially. "I mean, we heard something about a phone cord and glowing lights, but that can't be right. And my mom refused to say anything because of stupid confidentiality rules."

"And, you know, the law," Oliver said. We all snickered. "But I'd like to know too."

Oliver moved closer to me. The scent of freshly cut grass and laundry wafted from him, and I smiled. His steady, gentle presence after such a chaotic night felt like being wrapped in the coziest blanket.

"Well," I began, but Jenny leaned in.

"Let me tell them, Mom." Her eyes were bright despite her exhaustion. "You won't believe what happened with that phone cord. It was like something out of a sci-fi movie, but also kind of beautiful? And Mom's protection spell—"

"Ms. Matthews?" Detective Martinez's voice cut through the moment. "Could I have a word about a few things? I'll be in the library."

I sighed. "Rain check on the story, guys?"

"I should get going anyway," Calvin said, though he looked reluctant to leave. "But seriously, Jenny. Call the show sometime. Our listeners would love to hear about this. Or come by the studio and we can do an interview."

"About what happened tonight?" I asked. "I'm not sure that's wise at the moment. Perhaps the police want to keep the details private for a while."

"Or, you know, whatever." Calvin backpedaled quickly, catching my protective mom tone. "We can just talk about usual late-night paranormal metaphysical stuff."

Oliver reached for my hand and drew me slightly aside. "Are you sure you don't want me to stay?" he asked softly. "I could sleep on the couch in the library, keep an eye on things."

I shook my head. "Thanks, but I need to be here for Jenny. After everything that's happened..." I glanced at my daughter, who was still chatting with Calvin. "We have some things to figure out. I'll call you tomorrow, or, er, today, okay?"

He nodded, understanding as always. "I'll bring those donuts in the morning. Give me a call when you want me to come over with breakfast." He leaned in and gave me a soft kiss on the cheek. "Try to get some sleep. You definitely need it."

Calvin jingled his keys again. "Night, Ms. Matthews." He turned to Jenny. "I'll see you around, I guess. How long are you staying?"

Jenny shrugged, and smiled coyly. Hmm. Calvin's question was also on my mind.

I watched the two men leave, noticing how Jenny's gaze was fixed on Calvin's back. Well, that was interesting. Ah, youth.

"Honey, can you hang here for a few minutes while I talk to Detective Martinez? Then we'll figure out sleeping arrangements."

Jenny nodded, stifling another yawn. "Sure. I'll be right here." She gestured vaguely at one of the armchairs in the lobby and sank into it, looking both exhausted and wired.

I headed toward the library, where Martinez was waiting.

She sat at my library table, her notebook and three pens — black, blue, red — spread out in front of her. The room still held a trace of lavender, though the magical glow had completely faded.

"Two things," she said as I settled into a nearby chair that was in her line of sight. "First, we found something interesting in Ben's phone. Apparently Nico was blackmailing him."

I leaned forward. "About what?"

"His previous stalking arrest. Ben was trying to rebuild his life, and Nico discovered his past. Ben had apparently stalked a few women. At least a few." Martinez swiped through something on her phone. "But here's where it gets interesting. We also found evidence that suggests Nico was doing this to others. Ben wasn't his only victim."

"That's what Ben told us."

"His notes app was full of details about people's weaknesses, secrets, as if they were things he could use against them. Like a little black book of leverage. He even used Ben to do his dirty work, made him steal items while Nico created distractions with his performances. The crystals, the pen, all of it was part of his system of control."

"Yep. And that tracks with what Adam told me about Nico's past behavior," I said.

Martinez closed her notebook cover. "Ben's confession about the sleeping pills checks out, by the way. We found the empty capsules in his jacket pocket. He really did want to ruin Nico's night, not kill him. The dosage wasn't all that much."

"But mixed with whatever was in that blue cocktail..."

"Dr. Yates will determine the exact cause of death, of course, but preliminary findings suggest the combination of substances triggered a severe reaction. I've seen cases like this before." She stood and yawned. "Sometimes karma has a way of catching up to people like Nico. Even if it wasn't the way anyone intended."

I thought about Ben, about how his attempt to stop a bully had gone so terribly wrong. About how Nico's own cruel manipulations had ultimately led to his downfall.

"When do you think your team will be finished?" I asked, glancing toward my apartment. "I have guests checking in tomorrow. Or rather, today."

Martinez checked her watch. "The CSI team needs another few hours. But your apartment will be off-limits until at least noon, maybe a little later. We'll need to document and photograph everything." She paused. "Do you have somewhere to stay tonight?"

I gestured vaguely around us. "Well, I do own an inn. We have an empty room or two upstairs."

We both smiled, the kind of tired smile shared between people who've had an impossibly long night.

"Sorry about the mess," Martinez said. "Crime scenes are never tidy. But we'll try to leave everything as close to normal as possible."

I thought about the broken glass, the spilled blue cocktail, the scattered herbs under my desk. "Normal" felt like a relative term at this point.

"If you don't need anything else from me, I think I'll try to get some sleep." I stood, feeling about a thousand years old.

"No, we're good for now." Martinez gathered her tablet. "Get some rest, Amelia. Someone from my office will be in touch later today about next steps."

We said our goodnights, and I headed back to the lobby to collect Jenny. Time to find an empty room and try to process everything that had happened in the past twenty-four hours. Or hopefully, sleep.

I found Jenny dozing in the lobby armchair, her legs tucked under her. She looked incredibly uncomfortable, with a slight frown. She startled awake when I touched her shoulder.

"Hey, sleepy girl. Oliver put Freddie in a room upstairs so he wouldn't escape. It's nice, and clean. Want to crash there?"

She rubbed her eyes. "Yeah, sure. What about you, Mom?"

I shrugged, feeling the weight of the evening in every muscle. "Not sure I'll get much sleep tonight."

We walked upstairs and I unlocked the room, which was next to the one that had been intended for Nico. I flipped on the bedside lamp. Freddie was on the bed, grooming his stomach. He looked at us as if we were interrupting something important.

"Stay with me." Jenny's voice held a note of that childhood vulnerability I hadn't heard in years. "Please? The bed's big enough for the two of us."

How could I refuse? Besides, after everything that had happened, I wasn't eager to let her out of my sight.

Jenny collapsed onto one side of the bed, not even bothering to change out of her dress. I flopped down next to her and Freddie.

I arranged the fluffy duvet over us and settled on the other side then flicked off the light. Freddie positioned himself between us, his purr motor revving up.

Just like when Jenny was little and would crawl into my bed during thunderstorms, though back then we had a different orange cat. Hunh. I hadn't even made the connection between

Freddie and our old cat, Mittens, until now. They looked a lot alike. I let out a little laugh.

"What, Mom?" Jenny asked, her voice heavy with exhaustion.

"Do you remember Mittens? The cat we had when you were a kid?"

"Mmmm, not really?"

"Yeah, I guess you wouldn't. You were three or four, and he was quite old by that time."

Jenny's breaths grew longer.

I was sure she was asleep, and then came a soft, "Mom?"

"Hmm?"

"Can I stay here? In Cypress Grove? With you?" She paused. "I don't want to go back to Arizona."

"Of course you can stay. As long as you want." The words came out thick with everything I couldn't quite express in my exhausted state: relief, joy, that peculiar ache that came with watching your child find their way home again.

"Really?"

"Really." I reached across Freddie to squeeze her hand, feeling the slight tremor in her fingers that told me she was trying not to cry. Just like when she was little, except now we both pretended not to notice. "This is your home too. We'll have to tell your father, of course. But I'll deal with that."

After all we'd been through, sending a firmly worded email to Chad was easy-peasy.

Jenny shifted onto her side, facing me. "I had all these ideas, you know? Taking a year after graduating, maybe traveling around Europe with my savings. But after Sedona, after those lights, I didn't feel grounded. Everything shifted." She paused. "I need to feel safe right now. And watching you tonight, how you handled everything, how you protected everyone, I dunno. I've never felt safer than right here. There's something about this town, this inn, you being here. I want to stay. I get a good vibe. I promise I'll get a job and take classes and eventually graduate."

My heart swelled so much I thought it might burst. Here was

my baby, my little girl who once needed me to check under her bed for monsters, now trusting me to help her face actual other-worldly experiences. The weight of that trust, that responsibility, filled me with a fierce kind of bittersweet joy.

"Okay, sweetie. Don't worry about any of it now. Just go to sleep."

"Mmph. Thanks," she murmured.

Freddie's purr deepened between us, and I absently stroked his soft fur. In that moment, I understood something fundamental about motherhood. Heck, about being *a woman*, because you didn't need to birth a child to possess this special magic.

Our deepest purpose wasn't only to nurture or teach, but to create safety. Whether it was for our human children, our four-legged ones, or even an entire community. An entire world.

Women built safe harbors, ones where our beloveds could weather any storm, magical or mundane.

Jenny's breathing slowly evened out into the gentle bliss of sleep. But I lay awake, listening to the harmony of my daughter's quiet breaths and my cat's contentment.

Outside, the rain had finally passed, leaving behind the kind of stillness that only comes in the earliest hours of morning, after a fierce storm.

$$Epilogue$$

Two weeks later, I tightened the belt of my robe and sank deeper into the plush lounger at Crystal Waters Spa in Cypress Grove. The gentle sounds of Enya washed over me. I had thirty minutes to relax before my pedicure, and the massage I'd just had eliminated every accumulated knot in my back, making me feel like a limp noodle. Holy wow. This felt incredible after everything that had gone on recently.

The air was thick with essential oils, including lavender. The scent now reminded me of that strange, fatal, magical night with the phone cord, though this spa lavender was mixed with something citrusy and bright, perfect for a summer afternoon. The air inside here was the perfect temperature. Not humid, like outside, and not too air conditioned, like other businesses in Florida.

Jenny sprawled in the chair next to me, her face still glowing from her first-ever facial. She'd traded her shorts and T-shirts for one of the spa's impossibly soft terry cloth robes, her freshly massaged and pedicured feet tucked into cloud-like slippers. On my other side, Clara nursed a cup of goddess blend tea, her hair wrapped in a towel turban.

"I can't believe I lived near Boston all these years and never did a spa day. It was like I never bothered to indulge myself, and I don't know why," Clara said, reaching for an almond from a small dish on a table next to her. "I'm going to have to unpack that. Because the hot stone massage was like nothing I'd ever experienced."

"I had a psychic massage therapist," Jenny added. "She knew exactly where I carried my stress before I said a word. It was kinda freaky."

"That's Maggie," I said. "She's a coven member."

"Whoever she was, it felt incredible," Jenny said.

"Mmm-hmm," Clara murmured.

"We all definitely needed this," I chimed in, feeling a bit drowsy from my own chakra massage.

The past two weeks had been a whirlwind of life returning to a normal rhythm. Liz returned from her Alaskan cruise to help me with a daylong cleansing spell at the inn. We'd burned sage in every corner, hung protective crystals, and managed to erase all traces of that terrible night.

Well, almost all traces. Sometimes I still caught a whiff of lavender in the library near the desk, but that only reminded me of my successful spell.

Police Chief Christopher Wolf, Liz's boyfriend, gave me yet another lecture about getting too involved in crime-solving and demanded that I recount every detail of the evening (I could tell he was proud of the work Det. Martinez had done that night).

The showdown with Chad about Jenny's withdrawal from college had been exactly as explosive as I'd expected. But even my ex-husband couldn't argue with the economics when Jenny showed him the tuition rates for the local university, which were far lower than her school in Arizona. She'd already been accepted for the fall semester, (thanks to an assist from Oliver's connections in admissions), and the fact that she could live with me rent-free finally made Chad relent.

His only comment had been that Florida was "full of weirdos," which made me cackle. If only he knew. I refrained from saying something snarky in return, which I felt was an indication of massive personal growth on my part.

Jenny was starting work at The Enchanted Tome, the indie bookstore downtown, next week. The owner had been thrilled to hire someone who could manage their social media accounts, though I suspected Jenny was more excited about their extensive fantasy, science fiction, and metaphysical section. She'd been devouring books about UFO encounters, trying to make sense of her Sedona experience.

Fortunately, she hadn't been in contact with anyone — or anything — in the sky since arriving in Cypress Grove. It made me wonder if the town was some sort of place of protection for her, but only time would tell. For now, I had my eye on her and her moods.

Mostly, I was happy she was close by and that she seemed to be doing well. Jenny had met a few people close to her age around town, including Zoe, a reporter at the local paper. And of course Calvin Yates, but whenever I casually inquired about him, Jenny brushed me off with *"we're just friends, mom, sheesh."*

Clara was also doing well. We'd kept in touch as she'd settled into her new life on the Gulf Coast, though bureaucratic red tape was delaying her flower truck dreams. The permitting process was apparently more complex than she'd anticipated, but she seemed to be taking it in stride. Apparently the incident with Nico and Ben had reminded her that she was not only resilient, but capable of handling just about anything.

This weekend visit to Cypress Grove had been her idea, a chance to decompress and reconnect after everything we'd been through together. I was thrilled to guest her at the inn, and we'd spent last night at Grape Escape with Kristan, where Adam hosted a wine and cheese tasting. The whole evening had been hilarious and fun, and the three of us had hung out like lifelong friends.

"Oh, hey," Clara said, setting down her tea. "I meant to ask. How's Mitzi doing? I was thinking about her."

I smiled, remembering the city council meeting I'd attended last week. "She's actually doing great. She's launching a local program that helps seniors with their dental bills. Apparently that night inspired her to help others dealing with similar issues and she's applying for some grants. She's getting her dental surgery thanks to her MasterCard, though. Oh, and she's stopped drinking."

"Wait, really?" Jenny sat up straighter. "The same Mitzi who tried to teach everyone the Macarena?"

"The very same," I said. "Though she claims she doesn't remember that part. She did send me a lovely thank you note for, as she put it, 'preserving her dignity by tucking her into bed instead of letting her dance on tables.'"

Clara laughed. "And she had no idea about the magic phone cord or our citizen arrest of Ben?"

"None." I reached for my cucumber-infused water. "Though she did mention having an unusually peaceful sleep that night, despite everything. Said she had dreams about golden light."

"Speaking of that night," Clara lowered her voice, though we were alone in the relaxation room. "Has anyone heard anything about Ben?"

"Actually, I got a call from Detective Martinez yesterday," I said. "I meant to mention it last night, but we were too busy drinking."

"Mom! You were drinking?" Jenny made a mock horrified face. "Kidding."

Clara chuckled.

"Don't pretend to be scandalized, missy," I said, joking, then I turned to Clara. "The judge denied bail. Given his history of stalking and what happened that night, they're not taking any chances."

Jenny chimed in. "Thank God. That guy was a total menace to society."

"Definitely a relief," Clara added. "Though the whole thing is tragic, really. Two lives wasted. And what about all that stuff in

Nico's bag? Did they ever figure out why he was stealing things? Also the notes. What was the real purpose of that?"

"Oh, that's the other update," I said. "According to the detective, they found evidence that he'd been blackmailing several of his private chef clients, just like Ben alluded to. He'd take personal items during dinner parties, then threaten to expose their secrets unless they invested in his 'brand' or wrote glowing reviews. He even got some of the more tech savvy ones to give testimonials on social media. He had a whole racket going. That list we found on his phone? Apparently the 'useful' ones were targets for his blackmail. Oh, and by the way, we won't get our stolen items back for a long time. They're now evidence."

"I figured as much. But Ben and Nico, *wow*. What an evil team." Clara shook her head. "No wonder Nico had so many followers. He was extorting engagement. Like a mafioso, but instead of money it was for likes. Pathetic."

I snorted.

"The social media influencer version of Tony Soprano, but he was better looking and did it while shirtless," Jenny mused.

I squinted at my daughter. "That show is before your time."

"Mom, I've seen the classics. Come on."

The Enya tune that had been playing softly through the spa's speakers faded, replaced by a song that made me burst out laughing: "You Light Up My Life" by Debbie Boone. It was like some cosmic DJ was giving us a wink and a nudge.

"What's so funny?" Clara asked.

I wiped my eyes. "Remember? That lighter we found in Nico's bag? My aunt's Zippo? It had Debbie Boone's face engraved on it, with this song title? You Light Up My Life?"

"Oh right!" Clara began to giggle. "Ahh, Debbie Boone. I remember this song from when I was a girl. I was probably about six when it came out. That was a long time ago. Another lifetime."

"You're not kidding," I said.

"You still haven't told me who Debbie Boone is," Jenny piped up.

"Pat Boone's daughter," Clara said.

Jenny looked at us blankly.

"This song came out right around the time I was born, so it kind of predates me," I explained. "But my mother, your grandmother, used to sing it to me. Completely off key. I always thought it was tacky, but now I kind of love it."

"I do too," Clara said softly.

Jenny looked between us. "You Boomers and your cheese fest songs."

"Gen X!" Clara and I corrected in unison, then dissolved into laughter.

As Debbie crooned, the three of us continued to talk about 70s music, which somehow led to us trying to explain the popularity of the TV show, "Mork and Mindy" to Jenny.

"Robin Williams was a clueless alien, but had a heart of gold," Clara said.

"People really watched stuff like that?" Jenny asked.

"Heck yeah. Your Uncle Mike loved it. I was still little but I remember us sitting about six inches from the TV every week. You know, the big wooden console kind."

"No idea what you just said, Mom."

I grinned, and a sense of peace settled over me, the kind that comes from knowing justice was being served, that I'd made a new friend, and that my daughter was safe here with me in Cypress Grove.

"Did you have rainbow suspenders like Mork?" I asked Clara.

"You bet I did," she said.

"What?" Jenny looked from me to Clara, confused.

As I watched Jenny throw her head back laughing at Clara's Boston accent-tinged impression of Mork's various catch phrases, I knew that whatever mysteries or magic lay ahead, my daughter and I were going to be just fine.

— THE END —

THANK YOU FOR READING
TOTAL ECLIPSE OF THE HEX!
I'M SO GLAD YOU'VE CHOSEN MY SERIES TO READ.

IF YOU'D LIKE TO CONTINUE THE JOURNEY WITH
AMELIA,
FREDDIE, AND FRIENDS,
PRE-ORDER BOOK SEVEN IN THE SERIES.
RAIDERS OF THE LOST HEX
WILL BE PUBLISHED JULY 1, 2025.

Sweet Dotty's Depression-Era Cookies

(WITH AN ADDITION FROM AMELIA MATTHEWS)

From the gravestone of Dorothy "Sweet Dotty" Thompson (1895-1947)

Cypress Grove Cemetery, Row 7

During the darkest days of the Great Depression, Dorothy Thompson kept hope alive in Cypress Grove with nothing more than flour, sugar, and an unwavering belief that a warm cookie could lift any spirit. Known as "Sweet Dotty" to everyone in town, she found creative ways to stretch ingredients when sugar and butter were scarce, often trading her baked goods for eggs from local farms or vanilla from travelers who came from Cuba and beyond.

Legend has it that no child in Cypress Grove ever went to bed hungry during the Depression, thanks to Dotty's kitchen. She would leave baskets of cookies on porches at night, never taking credit, though everyone knew who their midnight baker was. When flour became too expensive, she worked as a laundress to earn extra money, just to keep her cookie operation going.

Before her death in 1947, Dotty insisted that her famous cookie recipe be carved on her headstone. "So I can keep feeding souls," she told her daughter. "Both the living and the dead."

Some say that on particularly difficult nights, the scent of fresh-baked cookies still wafts through the Enchanted Eternity cemetery.

INGREDIENTS

3 cups all-purpose flour
1 teaspoon baking soda
1/2 teaspoon salt
1 cup butter, softened
3/4 cup granulated sugar
3/4 cup packed brown sugar
2 eggs
2 teaspoons vanilla extract
2 cups chocolate chips
Lavender sugar for sprinkling (see recipe below)

INSTRUCTIONS

Sacred Preheating: Awaken your kitchen hearth to 375°F. Like the warmth of Dotty's generous spirit, let it prepare to transform simple ingredients into comfort.

Flour Foundations: In a bowl as deep as your compassion, combine the flour, baking soda, and salt. That's the trinity of structure that held Cypress Grove together through hard times.

Butter Blessing: Channel Dotty as you cream together the butter (or bacon grease, if you're feeling traditional) with both sugars until they become as light as hope itself.

Egg Enchantment: One by one, beat in the eggs. Follow with vanilla extract.

Mystical Merger: Gradually fold in your flour mixture.

Chocolate Charm: With the same care Dotty used to stretch precious ingredients, fold in the chocolate chips until they're evenly distributed through your dough like stars in the night sky under a New Moon.

Cookie Conjuring: Drop rounded tablespoons of dough onto ungreased baking sheets.

Lavender Blessing: If using Dotty's lavender sugar (interpreted by Amelia), sprinkle it over each cookie like magic dust.

Transformation Time: Bake for 9-11 minutes until golden brown, exactly as Dotty did during the Depression years, filling Cypress Grove with hope one batch at a time.

Final Rest: Let cookies cool slightly, their aroma mixing with the evening air just as it still does, they say, in the Enchanted Eternity Park in Cypress Grove.

Share the Love: Distribute these cookies as Dotty would: generously and with an open heart, remembering that sometimes the simplest gifts carry the most powerful magic.

Note: During the Depression, Dotty often substituted bacon grease for half the butter when times were lean, which some locals swear made the cookies even better. Amelia has tried this and sprinkled crumbled bacon bits atop the cookies instead of lavender. This yields a decadent, unique cookie with a sweet and salty flavor that is like catnip for bacon lovers.

LAVENDER SUGAR

(Amelia's Addition)

NOTE FROM AMELIA: My research at the Cypress Grove Historical Society suggests that Dotty would sometimes scent her sugar with local herbs and flowers. While her gravestone doesn't mention lavender specifically, I like to think she'd approve of this addition.

INGREDIENTS

1 cup granulated sugar

2 tablespoons dried culinary lavender buds (make sure they're food grade — don't poison yourself or your guests!)

INSTRUCTIONS

1. Place sugar and lavender buds in an airtight container
2. Shake well to combine

3. Let sit for 1-2 weeks, shaking occasionally
4. Sift out the lavender buds before using
5. Store in an airtight container

Note: *If you're in a hurry, you can pulse the sugar and lavender together in a food processor until the lavender is finely ground, then use immediately. But the slow method produces a more delicate flavor.*

Warning: *Use only culinary lavender. Decorative or craft lavender may be treated with chemicals not safe for consumption.*

(And if you're like Jimbo, our resident plant shaman, you'll want to make this sugar during the waxing moon for "maximum floral energy." But that's entirely up to you.)

Acknowledgments

"What we do today is what matters most. Let us rise up and be thankful, for if we didn't learn a lot at least we learned a little, and if we didn't learn a little, at least we didn't get sick, and if we got sick, at least we didn't die; so, let us all be thankful. There is no path to happiness: happiness is the path." — Buddha

Thank you to my readers. You bring me so much happiness, and I am grateful for all of you.

Tara's Titles

Crescent Moon Mysteries

Eat, Pray, Hex

I Want Your Hex

Every Hex You Take

Cattitude and Charms

Serving Up Hex

Total Eclipse of the Hex

Raiders of the Lost Hex

The Critters and Criminals Series

Gator Queen

Swamp Princess

The Coffee Lover's Mystery Series

Grounds for Murder

Cold Brew Corpse

Live and Let Grind

A Bean to Die For

www.ingramcontent.com/pod-product-compliance
Lightning Source LLC
Chambersburg PA
CBHW032257310726

48973CB00008B/2439